I0594100

TALON'S HONOR

THE AEGIS NETWORK: JACKSONVILLE DIVISION
BOOK TWO

JEN TALTY

JUPITER PRESS

This book is a work of fiction. Names, characters, places, and incidents are products of the author's imagination or used fictitiously. Any resemblance to actual events or locales or persons living or dead is entirely coincidental.

PRAISE FOR JEN TALTY

"Deadly Secrets is the best of romance and suspense in one hot read!" *NYT Bestselling Author Jennifer Probst*

"A charming setting and a steamy couple heat up the pages in a suspenseful story I couldn't put down!" *NY Times and USA today Bestselling Author Donna Grant*

"Jen Talty's books will grab your attention and pull you into a world of relatable characters, strong personalities, humor, and believable storylines. You'll laugh, you'll cry, and you'll rush to get the next book she releases!" Natalie Ann USA Today Bestselling Author

"I positively loved *In Two Weeks,* and highly recommend it. The writing is wonderful, the story is fantastic, and the characters will keep you coming back for more. I can't wait to get my hands on future installments of the NYS Troopers series." *Long and Short Reviews*

"*In Two Weeks* hooks the reader from page one. This is a fast paced story where the development of the romance grabs you emotionally and the suspense keeps you sitting on the edge of your chair. Great characters, great writing, and a believable plot that can be a warning to all of us." *Desiree Holt, USA Today Bestseller*

"*Dark Water* delivers an engaging portrait of wounded hearts as the memorable characters take you on a healing journey of love. A mysterious death brings danger and intrigue into the drama, while sultry passions brew into a believable plot that melts the reader's heart. Jen Talty pens an entertaining romance that grips the heart as the colorful and dangerous story unfolds into a chilling ending." *Night Owl Reviews*

"This is not the typical love story, nor is it the typical mystery. The characters are well rounded and interesting." *You Gotta Read Reviews*

"*Murder in Paradise Bay* is a fast-paced romantic thriller with plenty of twists and turns to keep you guessing until the end. You won't want to miss this one..." *USA Today bestselling author Janice Maynard*

BOOK DESCRIPTION

Talon Wilston has spent a lifetime asking for forgiveness and trying to escape his twin brother's shadow. His life is finally coming together. He mended his relationship with his twin and the rest of his family. However, there is one person whom he'd like to reconcile with, only she's been giving him the cold shoulder since their breakup. When an enemy from their past lands stateside, Talon vows to show Marley he's not the same man, except he's not prepared for the secret Marely kept from him all these years.

Marley Cole knew someday she'd not only have to deal with the aftermath of the mission that brought her and Talon together nine years ago, but that she'd also have to tell Talon the truth about his daughter. She'd been preparing for both for years. However, she never expected she'd be forced to do them at the same time, putting the two people she loved the most in the line of fire.

A NOTE FROM JEN TALTY

If you have not already read DELTA-MISSION by Kendall Talbot, please do so and check out Talon's twin brother's story! You will love Channing and Makenna!

For my friends on the river. Thanks for the inspiration!

WELCOME TO THE AEGIS
NETWORK

The Aegis Network is the brainchild of former Marines, Bain Asher and Decker Griggs. While serving their country, Bain and Decker were injured in a raid in an undisclosed area during an unsanctioned mission. Instead of twiddling their thumbs while on medical leave, they focused their frustration at being sidelined toward their pet project: a sophisticated Quantum Communication Network Satellite. When the devastating news came that neither man would be placed on active duty ever again, they sold their technology to the United States government and landed on a heaping pot of gold and funded their passion.

Saving lives.

The Aegis Network is an elite group of men and women, mostly ex-military, descending from all branches. They may have left the armed forces, but the armed forces didn't leave them. There's no limit to the type of missions they'll take, from kidnapping, protection detail, infiltrating enemy lines, and everything in between; no job is too big or too small when lives are at stake.

As Marines, they vowed no man left behind.

As civilians, they will risk all to ensure the safety of their clients.

A Note From Jen Talty

Some researchers have said there is a correlation between the ocean and being calm, happier, and more creative. Having spent a winter in Jupiter, Florida, I'd say these researchers are right on the money.

The SARICH BROTHERS series was born while I spent four months in Jupiter, walking the beach, visiting the Jupiter Lighthouse, driving around Jupiter Island, dining at various places on the water, and overall enjoying this next chapter in my life known as the 'empty nest.'

The Sarich brothers, while poor, had a good life, raised by loving parents. However, their father was killed in the line of duty when the oldest boy was just twenty and the youngest fourteen, changing their lives forever…

Each of the brothers struggle with a restlessness, in part caused by their father's death. They are strong, honorable, and loyal men. They aren't looking for a woman, as their jobs aren't necessarily conducive with long-term relationships. It's going to take an equally strong woman to rip down the Sarich brothers' defenses and help them settle their restlessness, so they can give their hearts.

The series does not need to be read in order, but the four novellas do follow a timeline.

Come join each of the Sarich boys in their journey to heal old wounds, mend broken hearts, and find their way to true happiness with the love of a good, strong woman.

I want to add that since this series has been released, and then re-released, my readers, have begged me to write Mrs. Sarich's story…well, it's coming! Look for Catherine's story, THE MATRI-ARCH, on January 14, 2020.

*Sign up for Jen's Newsletter (*https://dl.bookfunnel.com/rg8mx9lchy*) where she often gives away free books before publication.*

*Join Jen's private Facebook group (*https://www.facebook.com/groups/1917065479090470*), where she posts exclusive excerpts and discusses all things murder and love!*

Book Description

Ramey Sarich graduated from West Point Military Academy with honors and a broken heart. Swearing off relationships, but not women, he dives into his career as a test pilot for the Army. He's cocky and lives on the edge, but he knows he's the best test pilot the Army has ever seen. So, when one of the planes he's testing nearly crashes, he doesn't believe it was an accident. Wanting an outside source, he contacts his brothers, and they send help in the form of an ex-military female pilot now part of the AEGIS NETWORK. Ramey is prepared for anything, except Tequila Ryder.

Tequila Ryder has spent the last few years raising her half-sister's son. Now that he's settled in college, Tequila is eager to jump back in the field with the

AEGIS NETWORK. She's dealt with more than one arrogant pilot before; however, Ramey is anything but typical, and as she dives into the investigation, she can only come to two conclusions.

Either someone is trying to destroy Ramey's career.

Or kill him.

...together they unravel a twisted plot, while entangling their hearts, and falling hard. Hopefully they won't crash and burn both in the sky and in love.

*T*alon Winston had spent most of the last nine years trying to forget about two things.

The first one, his twin brother Channing and his girlfriend Makenna had finally absolved him for being the jerk he'd been most of his life—something he was working on, updating to the improved, less of an asshole 2.0 version. It was about time he grew up and stopped acting like a horny teenager all the time. He looked up over the folder and his heart melted a little. Channing and Makenna deserved a chance to find happiness without the past—and Talon's mistake—hanging over their heads.

The second had been Marley Cole—the only

woman who had the ability to twist his gut into knots, squeeze his heart until it hurt, and torture his soul without even batting an eyelash. She'd walked into his life and changed everything without even trying. Only, that change scared the crap out of him and he screwed it all up.

"What am I looking at? What is the Aegis Network?" Talon flipped through the classified documents from their mission in Colombia nine years ago where the incident between him and Makenna happened, nearly destroying his relationship with everyone in his family.

Marley hadn't been thrilled either. They had been together a time or two, but nothing serious, because he didn't do traditional girlfriends. He couldn't make the commitment. There were times he wanted to be with someone. To have that forever person he could count on, but he had no idea how to be the kind of man who settled down. Something different always came along and turned his head.

Marley hadn't been much different back then, and they enjoyed each other's company when it worked.

What happened in Colombia changed him fundamentally, though it would take a few years to force him to take a good look in the mirror and do the work to be the kind of person his brother and the rest of his family could be proud of, instead of expecting him to screw up.

The horror of it all still ripped through his heart. He'd never felt anything so gut-wrenching. Seeing Marley again made him want to be the dirty dog he promised himself he would never return to just so he could forget the pain. That thought didn't make any sense, except for the fact it would perpetuate the idea that he wasn't good enough. Deep down, he knew that wasn't true, but it had been the feeling he carried his entire life and something he didn't want to control him for another second.

"The company I work for," Marley said. She sat next to Talon. Way too close for comfort, wearing the emerald earrings he'd given her for her birthday. His mind floated back to that time in his life. He'd never been happier, yet there had always been this tickle in his brain that it would all blow up in his face and that's exactly what happened.

His feelings for her were as strong as they'd been six years ago, which was the last time they'd been in the same room together.

Channing and Makenna were across the fire pit. Makenna leaned close to Channing, looking over his shoulder at each piece of paper that Talon passed in their direction.

A tightness tugged at Talon's chest. Things hadn't gone well the last time he'd seen Marley. Since then, they only texted occasionally about Colombia. She always believed that trip was going to come back and haunt them. She warned Talon that something was evil in that kid's eyes as they flew away.

All Talon saw was a child.

"How does a private company have top secret documents?" Channing asked.

"Does it matter?" Marley pointed toward the file. "Our past is about to catch up to us and all our lives are at risk."

"I wasn't there," Channing said.

"Besides the fact you could be mistaken for Talon, Lopez has an agenda and it includes you." Marley leaned closer.

Talon scanned another page, doing his best to ignore how utterly beautiful Marley was. Even more gorgeous than he remembered. She didn't wear much makeup and her hair wasn't done in any fancy manor. As a matter of fact, she pulled it back in a ponytail and let it flow down the center of her back. She wore a pair of jeans that hugged her hips and a T-shirt that didn't leave much to the imagination.

"I can't believe he crossed the border." Talon glanced over the folder, catching Marley's gaze. Her piercing green eyes tore through his soul. Of all the women he'd known in his life, she was the only one who threw him off his game. She actually made him think about being a one-woman man. Then the shit hit the fan when he couldn't do the one important thing that would seal the deal.

That had been the single biggest mistake of his life.

Bigger than Makenna in many ways because Marley had been the key to his future.

"How did Lopez end up in the US?" Channing took one of the pages that Talon handed him and gave it to Makenna, resting his hand on her knee.

Too fucking cute. Talon was about to vomit over it. Of course, had Marley not shown up, he'd probably relish in his brother's happiness.

"Wait a second. Twin and her?" Marley cocked her head. "You two are together? After everything that happened?"

"My name is Channing and yes." Channing let out a long breath.

5

"Has she figured out how to tell the two of you apart so she doesn't end up in bed—"

"Shut the fuck up, Marley," Talon and Channing said in unison.

"Wow. She's one hell of a woman if she can forgive that." Marley leaned back.

Talon wanted to remind Marley that she forgave him for being a prick, but decided it wasn't the time or place to let his brother and girlfriend in on his and Marley's past on-and-off romance that had sucked the life out of him and nearly destroyed his soul. She'd been the best thing that ever happened to him and thanks to his inability to be a real man and a series of misunderstandings, everything went to hell.

"*Her* also has a name." Makenna lifted her hand and pointed to herself. "It's Makenna."

"Let's focus on the problem." Heartburn filled Talon's chest as if he'd swallowed an entire bottle of hot sauce. Marley hadn't liked Makenna from the second she jumped onto her helicopter. Marley didn't need Talon to explain what happened; it was written all over their faces. He might as well have had *I slept with my brother's girlfriend* tattooed on his forehead.

It was worse for Makenna.

6

Back then, Talon had a reputation for being a bad boy and a ladies' man and he didn't care. Marley accepted that about him because she wasn't looking for a permanent relationship. But taking his brother's girlfriend to bed crossed a line. He had no idea when he walked into that room that she might have mixed him up with his identical twin when he used his last name, instead of his first. He'd never met his brother's girlfriend. Barely knew he had one. It wasn't until after the deed had been done that they both realized their horrible mistake. "Just because this kid rebuilt his family's business and is in this country, doesn't mean he's coming after us. He was a small child when we flew out and the intel I have is that he didn't have a clue as to our identity. He saw a chopper fly out. He might not even know who was in it. I killed his entire family. The entire cartel. No one left could identify me, Marley, or Makenna."

"Except him." Marley stood and paced. The woman was high-strung, sarcastic as fuck, which he liked, and her instincts were also rock solid. She'd been an excellent helicopter pilot in the military. Her ability to think fast was invaluable in the field. She was an asset to any team. Talon knew he could trust her with his life.

Just not his heart.

"He was a kid." Talon glared.

"I wasn't suggesting you should have offed him," Marley said. "But I've spent a few years poking in places none of you can," Marley said.

"How is that possible? I have a pretty high security clearance." Makenna eased into one of the chairs and lifted the folder from Talon's hands. "Where the hell did you get this? These are top secret. Even I wouldn't have access to these. Maybe a five-star general could get them, but only if he has a reason."

"Working in the private sector has its perks," Marley said. "My bosses know a lot of people in higher places. Add in all the men and women I work with and their connections, and we have a network that spans the globe. Anyway, I've been collecting data on our little friend. He couldn't have rebuilt and expanded the family business as fast as he did, without the sophistication and contacts available in this country. Someone had to have helped him do that."

"We all know Makenna's operation was compromised by misinformation given about the Lopez organization," Channing said. "A mole that came from the inside."

8

"My men died thanks to bad intel during that rescue mission." Talon rubbed his temples. He didn't want to be reminded of all the death surrounding that mission. Good men were killed and he still felt responsible. His job had been to get his team behind enemy lines safely, rescue the asset, and get out.

That mission nearly destroyed his career.

His relationship with his brother and his family.

And it helped seal his fate with Marley. Their fights often circled back to what happened at his uncle Henry's funeral when he blurted out for the whole world to hear what he and Makenna had done. It wasn't so much that the truth had come out. That had been a necessary evil. But Talon had been drunk and he did it more out of self-destruction than anything else.

"Your sources really believe he's in this country for revenge," Makenna said.

Marley nodded. "Long story short, we had an assignment that dealt with his organization and one of our agents overheard Lopez mention Talon's name and wanting to make him suffer much in the same way he did. Specifically, taking out his family, one by one, leaving him alone, with no one."

"That's not good," Talon said under his breath.

9

"The Aegis Network is willing to put a team on everyone in your family. It means coordinating some things, but we also don't feel we should tell everyone they are in danger."

"Can you imagine what Aunt Betty would do with that nugget." Channing stared at Talon. "I agree with Marley on keeping the family in the dark. We don't need mass panic."

"We also don't think it's a good idea for twin—"

"Jesus, Marley, why must you call him that?" Talon let out a long breath.

She arched a brow. "Fine. We'd like Channing and Makenna in a safe house since they are the biggest targets. The ones who matter the most. Along with my daughter—"

"You have a kid?" Talon stared with his mouth gaping open. "You got married?"

"That surprises you?" Marley narrowed her stare.

"Hell yes, it does." He slammed the paperwork onto the chair on the other side of him and jumped to his feet. He had no right to be mad. He no longer had a claim to Marley. None at all. They started out as friends with excellent benefits. She'd been totally on board with that.

Until she wasn't.

He walked away.

He came back.

It didn't last.

All because he couldn't get the words out. He tried. He stumbled over his tongue. It twisted and grew thick and heavy, making it impossible to speak. It wasn't that he was incapable of change. He'd already done the heavy lifting. He'd given up his wild ways when it came to women. That was easier than he thought it would be.

It wasn't the emotional commitment he struggled with—or the ability to show it.

However, he couldn't say it.

Talon had a lot of regrets in his life, but that had been biggest one.

Marley had enough of him and tossed his ass out, again. Three months later when she came knocking on his door, she got the totally wrong impression about a compromising situation she found him in and that was the end of that. The only time he heard from her was a random text about Lopez.

But the text from Todd made Talon realize he wasn't properly suited for being Marley's life partner.

"What are we missing in this conversation?" Channing asked.

"Nothing," Marley and Talon answered at the same time.

"What about your husband? Doesn't he need protection too?" Talon reined in his jealousy that slipped out as anger. At least he knew what it was this time.

"He died last year in a boating accident."

"Shit. I'm sorry." Talon sank back into the chair. He took her hand and squeezed. "That has to be hard."

"I'm a survivor." Marley shrugged free. She shifted her focus to Channing. "Would you and Makenna be willing to go into a safe house with my daughter while Talon and I go on the offensive? I don't mean just go after this guy and put his organization out of business, but go after the mole from nine years ago because I bet whoever has been helping him set up is the same person who fucked us nine years ago and they want to do it again."

"It's not like my brother to sit on the sidelines," Talon said. "Can't we put one of your guys with Makenna?"

"I wasn't sure how this would play out, but I think it would be better to have them together. We'll need them to go over the intel. To look at the data coming in, especially potential leaks and threats. However, I hoped this could all be on the down-low." She pulled her long ponytail over her shoulder and ran her fingers through it. "Is there any way both of you can take a leave of absence or something? We need you off-grid for this to work."

"I'm on vacation now," Channing offered. "Two weeks to be exact."

"Me too," Makenna said. "We weren't planning anything out of this world. We could pretend to be on a trip and care for your daughter. How old is she?"

"Five."

"How long were you married?" Talon asked. He needed to know if what he was thinking was true and if it was, it would be even harder to remain calm.

"We're getting off task." Marley stood. "Holiday, the man who runs the Jacksonville office, sent a man to Miami, where we believe Sergio Lopez is currently hanging out."

"That's a day's drive away." Talon leaned back and rubbed the scruff on the side of his face, doing his best to file the fact that Marley had married and had a kid. She had every right to move on. She'd made it clear that she didn't believe a zebra could change his stripes. However, Marley was also a creature of habit. Either she went back to Todd.

Or she did the same thing she'd done in the past and found a warm bed to drown her pain in.

"Where do you want us to start?" Talon asked.

"First, we get Channing and Makenna settled in the safe house. Then we take over for the agent in Miami." Marley held his gaze. "Thank you."

"For what?" Talon narrowed his stare.

"I wasn't sure you'd agree that this was the kind of threat that warranted such an action, especially since all we have to go on is what my colleague overheard." Marley gathered up all the paperwork she'd brought and stood tall.

Talon eased off the chair. He had a good three inches on Marley, but she always impressed him by the way she held her ground in any situation. "From what you've presented, any reasonable ranger would assess that as a high-level threat."

"I concur," Channing said.

Makenna inched closer to Marley. "I've looked into Lopez and I've never gotten the kind of information that you presented. I'm—"

"It's all the real deal," Marley said with a sharp tone.

"I wasn't denying that." Makenna nodded. "If any of those documents had come across my desk, I would have reached out. You have my word that Channing and I will protect your daughter and whatever it takes to take Lopez and his cohorts down once and for all."

"Thank you." Marley's eyes glossed over and the corners of her mouth tilted upward into a half smile.

Damn.

It was rare he ever saw that kind of emotion. She had no problem expressing anger or passion. But anything in between those two things didn't come easily to either one of them.

"Are you all willing to leave first thing in the morning?" Marley asked.

"Where are we going?" Makenna asked.

"A little town called Jupiter about four hours south of here." Marley fiddled with her nails. She only did that when she was nervous about something.

"We can make that happen." Channing took Makenna's hand. "We better go inside and start making excuses for leaving so we can go pack."

"Go ahead. We'll be in shortly." Talon gave his twin one of those all-knowing looks that they often shared.

Channing nodded.

Talon had never been good at having deep discussions with women. Actually, he sucked at them. But Marley had been different. From the moment he met her, she'd made him feel as though he could be vulnerable. He told her things about himself that he never told anyone.

"I guess I know why you've ghosted me all these years." He folded his arms across his chest. "How long after you showed up at my apartment did you get married?" He suspected he knew the answer but wanted to hear it from her lips.

"Does it matter?" She tilted her head.

"Yeah. To me, it does."

"Six months," she said.

A sharp pain pushed through the center of his stomach. It twisted and turned as if someone were trying to cut out his guts.

"Todd?" He closed his eyes as he waited for the answer.

"Yes," she whispered.

"I shouldn't be surprised. You and he had a history long before I came into the picture." Talon blinked. He reached out and curled his fingers around her biceps. "I'm sorry for your loss." Todd wasn't the worst man in the world. Talon knew he cared for Marley, but he didn't love her the way Talon had—did.

"Thank you, but we divorced a year after we married."

"That still must be hard on your daughter."

She lowered her gaze and nodded.

"Hey." He took his thumb and lifted her chin. "What aren't you telling me?"

"Dylan Sarich, the Aegis Network agent who first overheard Lopez talking about you, also knew my daughter's name."

"Fuck, Marley. Nothing like burying the lead." Talon dropped his hand and let out a long breath. "If he's trying to make history repeat itself, he's coming for us and she'll be the one left standing."

"That doesn't make me feel any better," Marley said. "But there's more. However, I don't want to talk about it here. Can we go somewhere private?"

"Now?"

"If not tonight, can we meet in the morning before we leave for Jupiter? It's important. And it has to be just you and me."

"Okay. Why don't we have breakfast at Tunny's."

"Perfect. Thanks," Marley said.

Talon curled his fingers around her biceps, leaned in, and kissed her cheek. "See you in the morning." He turned and strolled off toward the front of the house with his heart in his throat and his mind in the past.

He still loved Marley. A fact that would never die.

arley Cole palmed her mug of coffee and stared at the black liquid. A thick gray line of smoke snaked up toward her face, bringing a bitter scent. It hit her nostrils, forcing her mind to sharpen and be alert.

Talon sat across the booth, fiddling with his cup. They'd been in the diner for all of ten minutes, but it felt like ten grueling hours. The thick tension between them grew stronger by the second. Their history hung over her head like a storm cloud, ready to unleash a powerful storm.

He tapped his finger on the table. He lifted his gaze and tilted his head.

God, she hated that look. He used to give it to her all the time when they'd be doing something that required patience, something that she didn't have much of unless it was in the field.

She should have all the calmness inside because, technically, she was on the job. She needed to tell Talon about their daughter, and she wasn't sure this was the right place, but what choice did she have? She couldn't wait until they got to Jupiter and she couldn't do it in the car on the way down in front of his brother and Makenna.

Last night, she'd lost her nerve. He'd been surrounded by his family and while that might give him the support he needed to deal with the revelation and keep him from losing his shit, she wanted privacy to explain her reasons.

"You called this meeting." Talon lifted his cup and blew into it before taking a long, slow sip while holding her stare with his bright-blue eyes.

There was a time when that gaze could melt her heart into a million pieces. Tallie had her father's eyes. Same color. Same shape. Every time she looked at Tallie, she was reminded of the only man who had captured her soul. She did her best to settle her emotions. "I need you to promise me you won't raise your voice, slam your fist on the table, or run off."

"When it comes to you, I can't do that." He

leaned back and folded his arms. "For the record, the last time we saw each other, you were the one who acted like a raging lunatic."

"That's a stretch."

"Really?" He tapped his forehead near the hairline. "You tossed a book at my head."

"You behaved like a condescending asshole."

"I'll give you that, but you didn't let me explain why she was there."

Marley let out a dry laugh that sounded like a dying animal. "That woman waltzed out of *your* bedroom, wearing nothing but *your* robe and a fucking smile on her face. I don't think that needs an explanation. I believe *that* message is loud and clear."

"Stacey did that to piss you off." Talon pushed the napkin to the side and leaned forward, resting his elbows on the table. "The two of you never got along and I'll agree she's a manipulative wench."

"You've got both of those statements right. But she was your go-to fuck buddy, and she didn't like it when you became exclusive with me. She constantly antagonized me and enjoyed rubbing your wild sex life in my face every chance she got."

"I won't deny that she was a total bitch to you,

but for a few months, before we broke up, she left you alone."

"That may be true." Marley waggled her finger. "But you went right into her open arms the second things got a little rough. You couldn't admit that you might be in—it doesn't matter. You went right back to your old ways without skipping a beat. When I showed up that day—which, by the way, you're the one who told me to come to your apartment—I realized that you would have been miserable if we stayed together. It's not in your nature to be in a committed relationship."

"That's the pot calling the kettle black."

"Are you serious? I've always wanted to settle down. I told you from the very start that I wanted to find the right person. The perfect match. Someone who understood me and would support my career. You know how hard it is to be a woman in the military; it's just that we were young and I wasn't in a hurry."

Talon chuckled. "I'm sorry. I don't mean to laugh. I don't actually get what that's like for you, but yeah, I've seen what you've been through and you don't deserve what some jerkoffs put you through. You're the best at what you do and I'm sure you're top-notch in this new organization."

No matter what she and Talon fought about, his unwavering champion of her ability to hold her own in a man's world humbled her. Not once did he ever make her feel as though she didn't have what it took to cut it in her chosen profession. "Thank you, but it doesn't change the fact that you slept with Stacey."

"But I didn't."

The waitress approached. "Are you ready to order? Or do you need a few more minutes?" She topped off both coffees.

Thank God for small favors. Marley needed a few moments to process his declaration. "I'll have French toast and crispy bacon."

"I'll do the same, but can you add some sausage, scrambled eggs, and crispy home fries." Talon lifted both menus off the table and handed them to the server. "Thanks."

"Coming right up." She turned and scurried off to the next table.

Marley stirred a few ice cubes from her water into the scalding liquid. She needed something to focus on. "You honestly expect me to believe you and Stacey didn't have sex the morning I came over."

"I've got no reason to lie now."

He had a point, but she didn't want to admit it, much less accept it. "I know what I saw."

"I won't deny she was there. Or that she'd spent the night. Or even that she had come out of my master after taking a shower." Talon let out a long, slow breath. "She wanted to get back at both of us and she thought that would do the trick, which it did."

"What the hell are you talking about?"

Talon ran a hand down his jaw, his thumb and forefinger stopping at the tip of his chin. "I ran into her two days before I was being deployed. She was there with some new man. We exchanged bullshit pleasantries. She tossed this guy in my face as if to make me jealous. It was comical because I didn't give a shit. I didn't want her. I texted you from that bar, giving you my schedule, and begged you to respond."

"Talon, this has nothing to do—"

"Let me finish." He raised his hand. "Three days after I returned from that mission, she showed up. She was upset. She told me that guy she was dating hit her. You know that's a hot button for me."

"Shit," Marley whispered. "I don't wish that on anyone."

"Well, it wasn't true." Talon sighed. "And I'm not the one who texted you back. She did, but I tried to tell you that and you didn't believe me."

"Would you have in my shoes?"

"Considering it was Stacey, I might have heard you out." He rubbed his temple. "You said you married Todd six months after we broke, right? That means it would have been roughly three months from that morning."

Her heart stuck in her throat. "I was pregnant."

"Is that the only reason you got married?"

She nodded. If she didn't spit it out now, she'd lose the chance. She stared him in the eye. A single tear burned her cheek. It dripped off her chin and onto the table. "But Tallie wasn't Todd's. She's yours."

3

*T*alon blinked.

There was no fucking way he'd heard that correctly. "What the hell did you just say?" He pressed his hands on the table and tried to suck in a deep breath. His lungs did not inflate with oxygen. They burned as if a raging fire had ignited.

"I know I should have told you, but—"

"Are you telling me I have a daughter who you gave my childhood nickname to? And that you never planned on telling me about her?"

"I came to your house that morning because I wanted you to know. Todd encouraged me—"

"Don't fucking mention his name to me." Talon shouldn't speak ill of the dead, but right now, Todd was no better than Stacey in his eyes. "He didn't want us together any more than Stacey did. He would have done anything to break us up. Hell, he did things to ensure we didn't get together. And he helped keep my kid from me." That damn fucking text that Todd had sent. It was worded that at first glance, he came off sounding as if he were simply trying to protect a friend, but in reality, the statement was more about telling Talon to stay away. That Todd would take care of her from now on.

Fucker.

The server came over with their food, placing it gently on the table. All Talon wanted to do was pick it up and toss it across the room.

"Does she have his last name?" Talon choked on the question.

"No," Marley said. "Her full name is Tallie Pearl Cole."

"Jesus fucking Christ. You gave her my grandmother's name for a middle name? I'm sure Todd loved that. I can't believe he supported this when he texted me to stay away from you after that incident with Stacey."

"He did what? I didn't know the two of you spoke," Marley said with a scratchy voice. It always twitched like that when she felt vulnerable.

He hated to hear her sound that way. Especially

right now. "I wouldn't say we spoke. It was one message from him. I never responded."

"What exactly did he say?"

"Something to the effect of: *I'm sorry that things ended this way between you and Marley. I honestly thought it would work out this time. She's really hurting right now and I think it's best if you keep your distance. She needs time to heal. Please don't try to contact her. I'm sorry, but this time, it's truly over. She's moving on. You should too.*" Talon stabbed his eggs and shoveled half of them into his mouth. He was sure they tasted fantastic, but everything felt bitter. "I struggle to believe that Todd knew she was mine and he was fine raising her as his own."

"It wasn't like that."

"Okay. Enlighten me then." He lifted a slice of bacon and tossed it in his mouth. "Because it sounds like the two of you got to play house while I was completely in the dark. We've texted a few times a year about Lopez and you didn't think to mention that I had a kid."

"Of course I did." Marley shoved her plate aside. "Todd always thought I should and we didn't get married because we had deep feelings for each other. I was still in the military. I was pregnant. You know how that goes. He helped me save face until I could get out, and we then went our separate ways. Todd was like a favorite uncle in Tallie's life. He wasn't her father, ever."

"If she didn't think Todd was her father, then who?" Talon's mind raced with a million questions. He tried to categorize them but couldn't. They went off in his brain like fireworks. He wanted to know so many things about Tallie—about his child—but he held on to his anger over the situation and couldn't bring himself to ask for the one thing he wanted more than anything.

A picture.

"You."

"Excuse me?" He swallowed. Hard. "She knows me? She knows I'm her father? You told her about me?"

"I should have done this a long time ago," she whispered. "I made a promise to Tallie I'd bring the two of you together as soon as it was possible."

"You have no idea how hard it is for me to sit here, look at you, and not toss a bunch of superlatives and maybe a few plates. It makes no sense to me why you wouldn't tell me."

"Are you kidding me?" Marley lowered her chin. "Besides constantly reminding me that you weren't a family man and that children were never on the table."

"I was softening on that."

"You never shared that with me."

She had a point. He tended to keep his thoughts about their relationship to himself until he was sure he was ready. "I get I screwed up a lot, but this is different."

"So is Stacey telling me that morning what a psycho I was and that someone with anger issues like me should never be allowed to be a mom."

Talon vaguely remembered that exchange and a few other digs Stacey had made that were totally out of line. After Marley left, he had a few choice words for Stacey, who continued with her belief he was better off without the unhinged helicopter pilot in his life.

"You didn't tell her to shut up. You didn't defend me. You let me leave," Marley said with a guttural sob.

"It was a volatile situation and I wanted Stacey out of my apartment and life for good," Talon said. "For the record, I did reach out and you know that. But you continued to ignore me."

"Because of this." She tapped her cell and

pulled up a few pictures and pushed her phone across the table.

He lifted the electronic device and studied the images of him and Stacey in what could only be described as a romantic embrace. He pinched the picture, zooming in. "These were taken before you and me."

"I didn't know that."

"Where did you get them?" He set the phone down. A dull ache formed between his temples. Stacey hadn't give up after that morning in his apartment. Nope. She'd come at him three other times.

"Where do you think?"

"And you believed her?"

"She told me she was pregnant." Marley sighed. "I learned it wasn't true. Each time I reached out to you, I wanted to tell you. But something always got in the way. Either it was something with you, or something with me."

"Those are all bullshit excuses."

"I know," she said. "I've had almost six years to think about everything that went down and I believe that Stacey manipulated everything that morning and continued to make sure we never got back together."

"I won't argue that point." Talon tapped her phone. "Are there pictures of Tallie on this?"

Marley scrolled. "Here's a recent one of her fishing. She loves it."

"She's five?"

"Yes."

He held his breath as he stared at a little girl with his eyes and Marley's long wavy hair. He could see a good mix of both of them in Tallie. "She's beautiful."

"She has your stubbornness."

"That's rich coming from you," he said softly. "What have you told her about why I'm not in her life?"

"That you're a ranger and your job takes you away a lot, but mostly that I made some really big mistakes and I need to bring you back in because I'm the one who kept you away."

"So she doesn't hate me?"

"I've told her nothing but good things about you. If anything, she resents me, but she's young. She's resilient."

"That doesn't make me feel better." Talon went back to his food. He didn't have a desire to eat, but his body needed nourishment. It was going to be long drive down to Jupiter and he sure as hell didn't want to do it on an empty stomach.

"I'm sorry," Marley said. "I can't go back and change the past. However, moving forward, I'd like for you to be in Tallie's life."

"Would you have told me now if Lopez wasn't in this country?" He struggled to forgive. He knew he was going to have to. An innocent child was at stake. One he had already fallen in love with. He held up the picture and his heart melted. All he wanted to hear was her sweet voice call him daddy.

It was a weird emotion to feel so tightly against his chest.

"Yes," she said with conviction. "For the last few years, I've been living and working in Orlando, but I asked for a transfer to Jacksonville, where your family is, because I want Tallie to know them. I'll be moving in a couple of months. Lopez pushed me into doing this in such a way that probably wasn't the best; however, it's out in the open now."

"Aunt Betty's going to hate you."

She laughed. "Does Aunt Betty like anyone the first time she meets them?"

"*H*ow are you holding up?"

Talon glared at Marley. His stomach churned. "I can't believe I'm a father." Talon tried to swallow his anger. He and Marley had more going against them than they had going for them. Even after being stationed again on the same base seven years ago, no one wanted to see them get together.

Todd constantly ran interference.

Stacey was even worse.

Then there were Marley's friends who thought he was a womanizing pig—which wasn't a total lie, but Marley had changed him and he'd never been the same since.

Tentatively, Marley curled her fingers around

his biceps and tugged him toward the front door of the safe house. It was a nondescript Floridian modular home on the Intracoastal Waterway right in the town of Jupiter. Marley told him that it was originally owned by the Sarich family, who worked for the Aegis Network, and now was used for situations like these.

"What the hell am I going to say to her?" He glanced over his shoulder at Channing and Makenna, who would come in after he'd had a chance to spend a few minutes alone with his daughter.

"You can try hello."

"Don't be a smart-ass," he said under his breath.

"I'm not." Marley leaned into him, hugging his arm as if she expected him to support her, not the other way around. "She's not a shy or quiet girl. She'll direct the conversation. I'm sorry that it will be short, but we must hit the road soon."

"I want to nail Lopez so I don't lose another minute with Tallie."

"I want that too." Marley pulled out her cell and tapped the screen. "Hey, Tequila. We're outside."

"Tequila? Is that a code name?"

Marley laughed. "Nope. And the name fits the personality. She's an ex-Army test pilot. Her husband also grew up in this house and is also a pilot."

Before Talon could ask any more questions, the door opened. A woman with blond hair stood in the entryway.

A little girl held on to her legs. "Mommy!"

"Hey, pumpkin." Marley reached down and lifted Tallie into her arms and squeezed her tight. "Have you been a good girl?"

"Yes, ma'am." Tallie nodded, brushing her hair from her face. She turned and her lips parted. She gasped. "Daddy? Or Uncle Channing? Sorry. I don't know what swagger is yet so I can't tell you apart."

Talon burst out laughing. He shouldn't have, but it was about the funniest thing he'd ever heard. He cleared his throat. "Your uncle Channing will never have swagger like me."

"Tallie, this is your dad, Talon, whom you were named after." Marley kissed Tallie's cheek.

"Hi, Daddy." Tallie flung herself at Talon, wrapping her arms and legs around his body, hugging him as tight as her little muscles would allow.

For a brief second, he stood there, stunned. He patted her back, not knowing what to say or what to do next. He had five long years to make up for and he sure as hell wasn't going to do it in an hour.

"Thank you, Mommy," Tallie said with thick emotion lacing her little high-pitched voice.

Marley took a step back and swiped at her cheeks. Tears continued to roll down her skin.

Tallie palmed his face. "Tequila says we're going on an adventure."

Talon shifted his gaze to the woman he didn't know.

"We'll get into that in a few minutes." Tequila gave him a weak smile. "I don't like Channing and Makenna standing out in the street. Tell them to walk around to the backyard."

"I'll text them," Marley said.

Talon set Tallie on the ground. He thought she might be tall for her age, but he wasn't sure. Her eyes were even bluer than his, but they had a tint of green like her mother's when the sunrays streaming through the window lit them up.

And her smile was identical to Marley's. Kind. Sweet. Genuine. It was one of the first things he'd notice about Marley when they met. He'd been drawn to all the things that made Marley human.

Her quick temper. Her sarcastic wit. Her compassion for others. Her drive and determination.

However, back then, they both allowed other people to affect their lives in such a way that it interfered with their ability to maintain trust.

"My uncle is here too?" Tallie asked.

"He is, but I thought we'd spend a little time together first." Talon took her by the hand and led her into the family room where a few toys had been scattered about the floor. "I'll tell you all about swagger." He eased down onto the carpet. He couldn't take his eyes off the child.

His child.

His little girl.

He'd never felt so much love for another person.

He could hear his aunt Betty's voice screaming at him to get a paternity test, but he didn't need one. Tallie was his. It wasn't just how much she looked like him; he could feel it in his soul.

"Mommy says it can be tricky to tell you and Uncle Channing apart because you're identical."

"We are, however my brother is so much more serious than I am. He doesn't have a good sense of humor and he can't take a joke as well as I can."

"Is that swagger."

He smiled. "It can be."

"What else?"

"But we have scars in different places and I have one right here and Channing doesn't." Talon lifted his shirt, showing off three bullet holes he'd received last year.

"Is there more?" Tallie fingered his scars with her pudgy little hands.

"I rub my temples when I'm thinking like this." He went through the motions. "And Channing pinches the bridge of his nose like this."

She plopped herself down and squinted her eyes, as if to study him with every brain cell in her body.

"Are you worried about telling us apart?" he asked.

"Mommy says once I know you better it will be easy. But I've seen pictures and it looks like it will be really hard."

"Your grandparents sometimes struggled to tell us apart, but another surefire way is that I'm quick to react and Channing takes his time to answer."

"You mean you're like Mommy." Tallie flipped her hair over her shoulder and rolled her eyes.

"I suppose you could say that." This little girl was like no other child Talon had ever met. She was articulate. Smart. Honest. Not afraid to carry on with adults. "Are you in school yet?"

"Kindergarten, but Mommy said I had to take a vacation from it for a while." Tallie pouted. "She says she'll explain later."

"She's doing what she thinks is best for you."

Tallie nodded. "She promised me I'd get to meet you and here you are."

Talon smiled. "Are these all your—"

"We've got a problem." Marley came stomping into the room. "Tallie, go into the kitchen with Tequila."

"No!" Tallie jumped to her feet, stomping. "I'm staying with Daddy!"

Marley's face had panic written all over it. She folded her arms and squeezed her elbows. That was never a good sign when she did that.

He pushed to a standing position, lifting Tallie into his arms. "Let me talk with your mom for a second and I'll come find you shortly." He kissed her cheek, taking a moment to take in her strawberry bubblegum scent. It was so sweet and innocent.

Everything about this moment had been surreal.

All the anger he'd felt toward Marley had

subsided. It didn't matter. What was in the past needed to stay there. For the sake of their child, he would find a way to forgive and move forward.

He wanted to be a part of Tallie's life.

More than a weekend warrior dad. He wanted to be engaged. Present. It all started in this space and time by backing up Marley.

"Okay." She smacked her lips against his and wiggled down his side, running off across the small modular home.

"You're really good with her," Marley said.

"I'm a shiny new toy. I'm sure we'll have our fair share of disagreements." He ran his hand across the top of his head. "What's the—"

"We've got to move." Tequila appeared. "Now."

"What the fuck is going on?" Talon asked.

"We've got unfriendlies entering the neighborhood on foot, from both directions. I have no reason to believe they have anything to do with Lopez, but why else would we have men with guns flanking us from either side. Your brother and Makenna are already in a car."

Talon raced through the house, his heart hammering against his chest. He scooped up his daughter. "Let's roll."

"You and Marley should—"

"Marley and my daughter will be traveling with me. Channing and Makenna can run decoy. Period." Talon kissed Tallie's forehead. "Daddy's got you. Nothing to be worried about."

"This isn't a good idea. It would be safer if—"

Marley cut Tequila off. "He's right. They won't know who to follow. If there's a woman riding shotgun, they will want to follow that SUV, not one where everyone's hidden."

"I've got a better idea. Do you have access to any of the boats?" Talon asked.

"My husband is on that boat there. You can take it. He and I will take over the SUV and we'll reconnect once you are out in the ocean. He'll plug in coordinates on the GPS for you to follow." Tequila opened the front door and glanced out. "Go."

"Cover us," Talon said as he held his daughter close and raced across the street, Marley one step behind, weapon at the ready.

A man with a scruffy beard waved. He handed Tallie off.

"Hey, Tallie," the man said. "Are you being a brave little girl?"

She nodded. "This is my daddy."

"I'm glad to meet him and hope to spend more

time with him." The man set the girl down in the bow. "You know anything about boats?"

"Born and raised. We'll be fine." Talon nodded.

"The outlet can be tricky. Just stay to the starboard past the jetties and head south. I'll be in touch on the radio once we've secured the area. Gotta fly." The man jumped onto the dock and pushed the vessel off.

"I need you and Mommy to stay down, okay?" Talon had grown up in Jacksonville and spent his time boating up there. He understood the Intracoastal and all the rules of the water. His family had teased him and his brother about joining the Army over the Navy, especially since he loved being at sea. Part of him had only joined the Army to prove he could be as good as his brother.

Only, he was always in his perfect brother's shadow. The one who could do no wrong.

Tallie sucked in a quivering lip.

"It's going to be all right, sweetie." Marley lay down on the bow of the boat, cradling their child. "I know this is scary, but trust Mommy and Daddy."

Talon pushed down on the dual throttles and eased out into the small channel, heading out toward the Intracoastal and eventually the ocean.

He quickly studied the GPS. Until they got to the outlet, it was all low wake.

Shit.

He glanced over his shoulder. Both vehicles were already gone. The goal would be to pull whoever had possibly found them off his tail and keep them on Channing's, while he headed north for a short distance until he could lose them safely. Being out in the open water wasn't ideal.

But the threat had come from land.

He kept checking his surroundings; nothing appeared out of the ordinary. He gunned it as soon as he hit the outlet, headed five miles offshore, and then due south.

Marley wrapped Tallie in a couple of towels and eased her way to the console. "She's sound asleep."

"Does she know anything about what's going on?"

Marley sighed. "No, but she's incredibly smart and she's going to have a lot of questions for us."

"My anger toward you is still under the surface, but I do trust you with my life. I always have." He looped a hand over the back of the captain's chair. "Could there be a leak in your organization?"

"Anything is possible, but I doubt it. We pull our

men and women from the most elite teams and my bosses are picky as hell. You'd be someone they'd love to get their hands on because you have a strong sense of loyalty, but love to bend the rules."

"Sounds like my kind of organization." He checked the time. "I read through all those files again last night, searching for hints regarding the mole in Makenna's original mission and there are two names that stick out."

"Reno Flatz and Harlan Carter," Marley said. "The Aegis Network has looked into all their missions, both in and out of the DEA. Flatz is a loose cannon, but no one can see it. Carter's a different story. He's been written up more than once for insubordination and when he left the DEA, he did so on not-so-great terms."

"He works for an outfit similar to yours."

"I wouldn't go that far." Marley's arm pressed against his and she sighed. "There's something else that's bothering me."

He rested his hand on her shoulder and pulled her closer, pressing his lips on her temple. She smelled like salty sea air and peaches. There was always something intoxicating about Marley. He'd been drawn to her from the moment they met.

In the beginning, they were magic. Being friends

with benefits meant they didn't have any pressure. They understood each other and could come and go as they pleased. They respected each other's space and never once got jealous when the other entertained someone else.

Okay, he occasionally got annoyed and so did she. That's why they tried the whole relationship thing. And for a long time it worked.

Until he fucked it up.

"I'm guessing it's the same thing that crawled up my ass and died." The moon appeared in the darkening sky. He flicked on the navigation lights and powered up the spotlight, panning it port to starboard and back and again.

She pulled out her cell and set it on the dash. "We have no service this far out."

"Nope," he said. "We need to get rid of those." He pointed.

"Tequila, her husband, and another one of our operatives had been keeping an eye on the place. No one was lurking in the shadows. They showed up when we did."

"My mind has been thinking the same thing."

"It makes sense that I would come to you," she said. "I was careful. I took roundabout routes to get to you. I didn't use GPS. I did everything I was trained to do to make sure I wasn't followed."

"We both know we did the same thing today, and yet they waltzed in shortly after we got settled. The question is, how are they tracking us?" He took his phone and Marley's and tossed them overboard. "Any other devices?"

She wiggled her watch off her wrist and placed it in his hand. "That's it."

It landed in the water with a baby splash. He lifted his gaze. His daughter was curled up under the towels and lay blissfully asleep in the bow.

So precious.

Beautiful.

"I want to hate you for keeping her from me." He took Marley's chin with his thumb and forefinger. "I've been replaying that morning you came to tell me and I was as much of a dick as you were being a bitch."

"And then there was Stacey." Marley arched a brow. "Swear to God she got off on watching us fight."

"I don't disagree. She set it up in hopes I'd fall back into bed with her." He licked his lips, leaning closer. He'd never had control of his emotions when Marley was nearby. He tried to keep a lid on them, both good and bad, but it always proved impossible. She filled his heart full of love—and every other feeling a man could possibly have. "I'm sorry I didn't chase after you that day."

Marley palmed his cheek. "I should have told you I was pregnant, regardless of who was at your apartment or what I thought was going on. That decision has haunted me every day since."

"I want to be in her life." He pressed his lips over hers in a tender kiss. He kept it soft, sweet, and short. "I'm not the same man. I can be a good father."

*M*arley watched as Talon tucked Tallie into bed. He kissed her forehead and stood over her for a long moment before tiptoeing out of the room. The way he embraced being her dad without reservation warmed her heart. It didn't erase the guilt she carried for not telling him about his child. After hashing it all out, she realized how pathetic her reasons had been.

"Channing and Makenna will be here by morning," Charlie Black said as she leaned against the doorjamb between the kitchen and the living room. "They couldn't find any tracking devices in the cars, the house, or your belongings, including the kid's stuff."

"Thanks, Charlie." Marley worked on two

assignments with Charlie through the Aegis Network last year. Charlie was a badass fire protection specialist when she'd been in the Air Force. The Aegis Network was lucky to have picked her up.

"Anytime." Charlie nodded. "We've got this place covered. I'll be outside if you need me. We'll regroup with a new plan, and you should be able to hit the road by nine."

"When I retire, I think I might check out this organization of yours." Talon made his way across the small home and ducked his head inside the fridge, pulling out two beers. He cracked both open, handing one to Marley. "I know we shouldn't indulge, but finding out I'm a dad warrants one."

"Happy first Father's Day." She tapped the longnecks together and took a seat on the sofa in front of the secured laptop that Charlie had left. She fired it up and opened one of the files. She'd read through the documents a dozen times. Nothing stood out.

"She's a sweet kid." He eased onto the couch and glanced over her shoulder.

She searched for the two names she and Talon discussed on the boat. She kept her focus on work and not the man breathing hot air on her shoulder, reminding her of all the wild, passionate nights they shared. Their past relationship could never be described as a bad one, but it wasn't great either. They fought as passionately as they made love. Her problem had been his inability to commit. When he did, he refused to say the three little words that mattered most. She never understood why he couldn't do it. When she found out she was pregnant, she was scared shitless to tell him. She had three friends who had miscarriages and not that she wanted that to happen to her, but she waited until she got past the twelve-week mark before making the decision to tell Talon.

That was probably her first mistake.

Too much time had passed between their breakup and the morning at his apartment.

She blinked, forcing her thoughts back to the current problem. Her fingers scrolled over the trackpad.

Flatz still worked for the DEA. However, he was no longer a field agent.

Carter worked for a protection agency. He had three run-ins with the law since leaving the DEA. They weren't uncommon infractions in her line of work. There were a few times she had to grease a few palms to get out of trouble all because she had to bend the rules to get the job done.

However, Carter had been notorious for being insubordinate. That was an entirely different skill set that wasn't welcome at places like the Aegis Network. Asher and Decker, the founders of the organization, encouraged independent thinking. However, a direct order was still an order. Unless someone was going to die, you followed it.

"Tell me about her," Talon said. "I mean, I feel like I know her, but I don't really and I want to desperately."

Marley set the laptop aside. "That would take a few hours and the best way for the two of you to bond will be through time." She lifted the beer and sipped. "Every time I reached out to you, I honestly believed that was the time I was going to say, *hey, we need to talk. Let's meet.* But I always got cold feet. Or you mentioned you were deployed or about to go on a mission. I found a million excuses not to tell you because I was afraid."

"Of what?" He shifted, staring at her with his big blue questioning eyes. Behind them was a combination of hurt and anger and she put those emotions there.

She thought telling him would empty the guilt

she carried in her soul. She sighed. "At first I thought you'd reject her. Tell me she must be someone else's."

"We were a couple. You wouldn't do that to me. To us," Talon said. "I don't care that both of us had reputations for playing the field. We were committed to each other. We might have had problems, but that wasn't one of them."

"Thanks for that." Her heart fluttered, remembering all the good times, and there were many. Their relationship had been a roller coaster. One that spun upside down and had tight turns. It was exhilarating and horrifying at the same time.

He took her hand. "Did you honestly believe I'd turn my back on my kid? Do you really think that low of me? Or was it something else?"

Tears burned her eyes. She didn't want to cry. She hated when that happened, especially when it had to do with Talon. "I mean, at first I couldn't believe you went back to Stacey. I now know that's not true, but you didn't do much to make me believe otherwise. And then we just never talked after that."

"You made it crystal clear we were over." He arched a brow. "I know I'm not the easiest man to get along with. I've made a lot of mistakes in my life. I get that. But I would have done right by Tallie. By you."

Dropping her head back, she closed her eyes. The last six years filled her mind like a movie going in fast-forward. There were so many milestones she'd wished Talon had been there to witness. "I didn't want you to feel obligated and end up resenting me and eventually her." She blinked, shifting her gaze and placing her hand in the center of his chest. "I understand your heart better than most people. You've spent your life wanting to be *good enough* but feeling like you're always struggling to prove your worth."

"I've learned that's on me, not the rest of the world."

Twisting her body, she sat cross-legged. "I'm sorry. I will forever be trying to make it up to you."

He reached out, cupping his thick fingers behind her neck. "I'm not going to hold this over your head. I can't be angry at you. I said some nasty things that day."

"Oh. I remember."

"We really knew how to hurt each other." He tilted his head, licking his lips. "I should have been able to tell you that I loved you."

She jerked. Her pulse beat in the center of her throat, making it hard to swallow.

Loved.

It was past tense, but he said the words that she'd so desperately wanted to hear six years ago.

Jumping from the sofa, she paced in front of the coffee table. "That rolled off your tongue pretty easily." She wiggled her fingers. God, she missed flying a chopper. There was nothing like being up in the air. Just her, the blue sky, a few clouds, and the hum of the engines.

"I didn't mean to freak you out," he said with a hint of humor laced to his words.

She paused and glared.

Slowly, he rose and stepped around the furniture separating them, taking her by the hips. "There is no rational explanation for why I couldn't say it when I knew without a doubt it was true. I told myself that if I did, you'd laugh, pack up, and leave me, which is silly."

"No. That's a reasonable fear." She wanted to take a step back, put some distance between them, but instead, she found herself resting her hands on his strong shoulders. He'd been an easy man to fall in love with, but not an easy man to love. His past had a nasty habit of catching up with them and no matter how hard her heart wanted to believe he had changed, her mind couldn't wrap around the concept. "The longer I waited for the words, the more I knew we weren't going to make it."

He dropped his forehead to hers and cupped her face. "You don't know what you have until it's gone," he whispered. "I loved you then and I love you now."

Every muscle in her body froze. Her breath caught in her throat. "You can't just say that and expect me to fall into your arms again." The words hung in the air over her head like a thick cloud. She wanted them to coat her skin like a warm blanket, but all they did was needle her with the one memory that hurt her so badly that she couldn't shake. "When I told you that I loved you, all you did was take a step back, grab your keys, and mumble something about our plans later. When I said it again, you stared at me as if I had five heads. You proceed to kiss me as if that were an answer. I waited weeks for you to tell me and you never did. Saying it now doesn't change what happened."

"It doesn't make it any less true." He took a step back and shoved his hands into his pockets. "We have a child together. I have five years to make up for when it comes to Tallie and I want to be in her life. I also want to be in yours and as more than a co-parent. Not a day has gone by that I haven't thought about you."

"But not enough to reach out or fight for me." It all came down to one fact.

Talon had let her walk away.

"That's not entirely true." He shook his head and turned, reaching for his beer. He tossed his head back and took a hearty swig. "I called and texted you for weeks. You didn't respond."

"Your messages were—"

He held up his hand. "It doesn't matter anymore. We can't change what either of us did in the past that brought us to this point." He nodded toward the bedroom where Tallie slept. "I'm her father and you chose to keep me from her. I won't use it to hurt you; that will only hurt her. I'd also like to believe that I'm a much different man than I was six years ago. I'm going to spend every moment I can with her and that means you and I will have to learn to be in the same space. My feelings for you are just as strong as they were back then and that scares the shit out of me. I have no idea where to file them, especially since you obviously don't care about me that way anymore."

"Talon, it's not that—"

"Let me finish," he said. "Once we deal with Lopez and our daughter is safe, I want to sit down and discuss what co-parenting will look like. I will do whatever it takes to be in her life, even if that means leaving the Army and getting a job with the Aegis Network."

"You don't have to do that." She swiped the single tear that burned a path down her cheek. "I won't ever stop you from spending time with her again." She clutched her chest. "We should probably get some sleep. Our sources have confirmed that Lopez is still in Miami but plans to move his drugs in the next couple of days."

"We need to consider that's a decoy."

She nodded. "Let's discuss that tomorrow." She turned on her heel and headed into the room where her daughter slept like an angel. Quietly, she closed the door, but not all the way.

Sitting on the edge of the bed, she covered her face. Talon had professed his love and she shut him down. She told herself it wasn't the right place or the right time. However, the truth was that she couldn't bring herself to take the risk.

Tallie needed a father more than she needed to be in Talon's arms.

$\mathcal{T}$alon tossed—more like aggressively threw—his shirt across the room. He missed the chair in the corner and it landed on the floor. "Fuck," he mumbled. He undid the button of his jeans and raked a hand across the top of his head. "No. I'm not letting this happen again." He yanked open the door and stomped down the hallway toward the other bedroom. A noise in the kitchen caught his attention. He turned his head.

Marley stood in front of the fridge. She glanced in his direction. "I'm hungry, but nothing looks appealing." She shrugged, shutting the door.

He swallowed, trying not to gawk.

She wore nothing but a T-shirt and a pair of

panties. She tugged at the hem of her top, trying to pull it down toward her thighs. No one was as beautiful as Marley. Not in his eyes. Over the last six years, he'd compared every woman he'd dated to Marley. Not just looks but their ability to hold an intelligent conversation. Marley was the total package. She had everything going for her, and he'd been the fool who'd let her slip through his fingers.

Not this time.

"I've spent the last few years trying to be a better person and do you know the hardest part?" he asked.

"No, but I get the feeling you're about to tell me." She shifted her weight back and forth, doing a little dance on her toes.

"No one ever believes I've changed. No matter how much I show them I'm different, except maybe Channing, but even he acts like I'm going to fuck up eventually and I get it. I do. I've been second to my twin my entire life. Never quite good enough and when it comes to my love life, I can understand why any woman would be leery of dating me. However, ever since we broke up, I haven't been able to get you out of my head or my heart." He tapped the center of his chest as he inched closer.

He wanted to feel the heat of her body. "You know me better than anyone. The only reason I didn't come after you was because of that damn text from Todd. I knew in my heart that the two of you had gotten together. That you had done exactly what you had accused me of doing."

"That text was your excuse." She swiped at his hand and poked his chest. "You're too selfish and when you get butt hurt, you coil up like a coward."

"Well, I'm not doing that now." He wrapped his arms around her and heaved her to his body, holding her tight. "I'm here. I'm present. I'm telling you that I still love you and now I'm going to show you." He kissed her so hard he thought he might have bruised both their mouths.

Her tongue twisted and rolled over his in a familiar passionate dance. Her fingers dug into his shoulders. There was a sense of desperation in her embrace.

Smoothing down her thighs, he gripped the back of them and lifted her feet off the floor, keeping their mouths properly entangled. He stumbled to the bedroom, closed the door, and falling onto the mattress with her legs still wrapped around his waist.

God, she felt so good. His hands remembered every soft curve. She smelled like a meadow on a cool spring morning and tasted like a fresh picked juicy raspberry. He'd fantasized about what it would be like to be with her again and now that she was in his arms, he had no intention of letting go.

He'd prove to her he was now worthy of her affection.

His heart raced.

She might not love him anymore. It didn't matter that they were grappling desperately to remove the rest of their clothing. She curled her fingers around his length.

Dropping his head to the pillow, he groaned as she kissed the center of his chest.

Her tongue darted out from between her plump lips.

"Are you going to torture me?" he managed.

Glancing up, she smiled. "That's the plan." She continued down his stomach, which twitched with every tender kiss.

He tangled his fingers up in her long hair, pooling it on the top of her head. He watched as she slowly took him into her mouth. His lungs burned as he tried to suck in air and his toes curled.

Her hands and mouth worked together to bring

him the most incredible pleasure he'd ever experienced. Life without Marley had been hell and he never wanted to return to a world where he didn't have her in it and not as a friend or a co-parent; he wanted her in the forever way.

He always had, but he'd been too stupid to take hold of the best thing that had ever happened to him and run with it.

"That's enough of that." He tugged at her hair.

Seductively, she inched her way up his body, licking her lips. No one loved like Marley. She gave herself fully and with an open heart. His life had been empty without her and as he rolled her to her back, he vowed to himself he would find a way to have her in his arms forever. Not fighting for her had been the biggest mistake he'd ever made.

Not fighting for family had been the second.

Those two things would never happen again.

Ever.

He tasted her skin, not letting any part of her go untouched. He worshipped her body as if she were a goddess. He loved how his name rolled off her lips and landed on his ears. The way her hips lifted and her heels dug into the mattress while he teased her, bringing her close to orgasm with his mouth, but not over the edge.

"Please," she begged. "Talon, I need you."

It wasn't the words he wanted, but for now, it was good enough. He settled between her legs, taking her mouth in a hot, passionate kiss. She accepted him, arching her back and grinding. Their bodies connected like missing pieces of a puzzle. They knew exactly what the other needed and when. Being with her was like coming home and he never wanted to leave.

Deep inside his soul he knew he'd never be the kind of man he should be unless she was at his side.

Slowly, his breathing returned to normal. He rolled to his side, pulling the covers over their naked bodies, wrapping his arm around Marley.

She rested her head on his shoulder, her fingers dancing across his stomach and chest.

He had a family.

People he needed to protect. To love. In an instant his entire world changed.

"I'm going to take care of Tallie." He kissed Marley's temple. "And you," he whispered.

Her warm, sweet lips landed on his skin with a sizzle. She tilted her head. "I want you to always be there for Tallie. I do. But you and I have always loved hard and fought hard. I don't know if that's a good environment for a child."

Reaching out, he took her chin with his thumb and forefinger. He stared into her eyes, searching for the love he knew existed and he found it swimming in her gaze. She could keep the words locked inside and avoid saying it, but it was there—she still loved him.

His heart thumped in the center of his chest. He brushed his lips gently over her mouth. "We're different people."

"I don't want to get her hopes up about something like that," Marley said. "She's been looking forward to meeting you. Having you in our life like this only to be taken away would be cruel."

Talon supposed he could understand that train of thought. The last thing he wanted to do was hurt his daughter in any way. What he couldn't quite put his finger on was Marley questioning whether he'd be the first one to call it quits.

Or would it be her?

"We don't know what we could be together unless we try and truthfully, we've never given us an honest shot. Both of us always had one foot out the door. I think we owe it to our daughter and to ourselves to at least explore this and to be all in."

"We don't know each other anymore." She

clutched the sheet to her chest and sat up. "Being good in bed together doesn't mean anything."

"It doesn't mean nothing, either." He fluffed the pillow and leaned against the headboard. Part of him wanted to settle back down and save this conversation for later. This was dangerous territory and could lead to a fight.

However, if they got through this, he could show how much he had changed. How he wasn't such a hothead who stormed off all the time.

"I'm going to be in her life." He took Marley's hand. "Which means spending time with you. I want us to do things together as a family. We can have picnics. Go to the park. Go camping. Whatever she wants."

"You can do those things with just her."

He shook his head, pulling Marley into his arms. He kissed the top of her head, smoothing his hands down her back. "I know you, Marley, and I can tell you want to try. If you didn't, you'd already be out of this bed with your clothes on."

"Can we table this conversation until after we deal with the Lopez threat?"

"Sure." He wanted to say no, but he didn't want to risk losing her forever. "Let's get some sleep." Leaning over, he flicked the lamp off.

She rolled to her side, tucking her butt against his front side.

With his arms around her sweet body, he closed his eyes and imagined what life could be like as a husband and a father.

A slow smile tugged at his mouth.

7

*M*arley normally loved waking up
alone.

But not this morning. She padded down the
short hallway, following all the amazing smells. Rich
coffee, sizzling bacon, and cinnamon.

Shit. He made his signature French toast.

Of course, that's about all he knew how to
make in the kitchen. If he couldn't grill it, he
couldn't cook it. But he certainly liked to eat.

"Good morning," she said as if they hadn't
made love twice last night, although her cheeks
heated the moment she caught his gaze.

He stood in jeans and a T-shirt, holding a
spatula in front of the stove. "Hello, sunshine." He
smiled.

"Mommy!" Tallie waved her fork in the air. "Uncle Channing and Aunt Makenna are here."

"I see that." She took the cup of coffee that Makenna offered.

Tallie leaned closer. "You're right. Uncle Channing doesn't have any swagger and he's sooooo serious," she whispered. "It's going to be easy to tell them apart, even if they try to trick me."

"Our days of doing that are long over." Talon chuckled. "Besides, we always got caught. It was never worth it."

"Oh, that's funning coming from you," Channing said. "Whenever we did switch places, it always got you out of trouble and me into it."

Talon chuckled as he set another plate of food on the table. "It always caught up to me." He pulled back the chair, squeezing her neck as she sat down. "But you know, Tallie. Doing stuff like that with my twin was a bad thing to do."

Tallie waved her fork. "Not if it was a joke." She winked. "That could be funny."

"She is definitely your child," Makenna said.

Talon grabbed a wet paper towel and masterfully cleaned up Tallie's pudgy little fingers and her sweet little face as if he'd been doing it her entire life. He lifted her from the chair and gave her a big kiss on the cheek. "Can you go watch television in the other room so I can talk to the grown-ups?"

"Mommy? Can I?" Tallie asked.

"Sure, but remember the rules about what you can watch." Marley dug into her breakfast while she waited for the noise of Tallie's favorite children's program on the streaming app. "Do you have any information on who was at the safe house in Jupiter and how our location was breached?"

"We do and we don't." Channing stood, found his backpack, and pulled out a folder. "Makenna had some friends do a little digging. I contacted the Aegis Network who got together with Makenna's contact. They are following a few things together. But I'm getting ahead of myself."

"It's amazing you and Talon are identical." Marley lifted her mug. "Get to the point."

"I'm working on it." Channing placed a few papers on the table. "Since your phones are at the bottom of the ocean, we can't be positive, but we believe there was a tracking app on one of them."

Marley pushed her plate to the side and picked up a map of Jupiter. "What am I looking at?"

"The route we took when we left the safe house is this one." Channing tapped a page. "But those men didn't follow us. They went to the inlet."

"Mia Sarich, of the Aegis Network, and some people I know through the DEA," Makenna said, "have been working all the logical explanations on why this would be, but one of them would be checking out your phones. Since we can't do that, we need to know if there is any chance they could have been tampered with so Mia can work her tech magic."

"I got a new cell three weeks ago." Marley had cracked her screen and since she had insurance, she took advantage of the ability to upgrade to the latest and greatest. "But I was in Jacksonville when I did it, not Orlando."

Talon squinted. "Why?"

"I came to see you, but you weren't home," she admitted.

"But Lopez hadn't crossed the border yet." Talon shifted, resting his elbow on the table.

"I had gotten final word on my transfer. I wanted you to know about Tallie," she said under her breath. "On the one hand, it's possible that whoever was in that store could have been a plant; however, it wasn't my usual store or mall that I shopped in."

Talon rubbed his temple.

"What's bothering you?" she asked.

"I don't believe in coincidences." He pushed his chair back, stood, and gathered a few dishes. Talon had always been a tactile man. He had to keep busy. It was rare she'd ever seen him truly capable of relaxing. Whenever his mind moved, so did his body. "I ran into Stacey a few weeks ago."

"If I didn't already hate her, I do now." Marley swallowed. This woman kept coming back and haunting Marley's very existence. "Where, and I can't believe I'm going to ask this, but what happened?"

"I haven't seen her a couple of years, but it's always weird when I do." Talon pressed his hands on the counter and leaned forward. "It was at Bixby's Bar. I was hanging out with a buddy. Stacey strolled in with a girlfriend and plopped herself down next to us. I told my friend that he could have either of them, but I was walking out the door. I did so without my phone."

"Stacey had it?" Makenna asked with a scrunched nose.

When Marley had first met Makenna, she hadn't liked her because of the mistaken identity situation between Talon and Channing. Makenna had been in a relationship with Channing, and

Marley believed Makenna should have been able to tell the difference. Granted, it had been dark, emotions were running high, and Talon had explained numerous times he'd never used his first name, only his surname. That only proved to make Marley angier at Talon.

He should have been aware of Makenna's hint of recognition.

"How'd she get it? You guard that thing like it's a weapon," Marley said.

"I had it on the bar because I was waiting for a text from Channing. I didn't want to miss it, so I left it out so I would see when it came across the screen."

"You should have put that thing on vibrate," Channing said.

"I hate that." Talon stiffened his spine and folded his arms across his chest. "Stacey was leaning into me and being her normal obnoxious self. I tossed a twenty on the bar, said goodbye to my buddy, and left."

"Wouldn't you have seen your phone then?" Makenna asked.

"At the time, I figured she took it when she kept trying to shove her boobs at me, just in case I didn't take the bait. That way she'd have to show up at my place, which she did, with my phone." Talon ran a hand across the top of his head. "Only, now that I look back, she didn't worm her way in or try to seduce me. She took my cell out of her bag, told me she had no idea how she ended up with it, placed it in my hand, and left. I thought maybe she was playing a game, thinking I would chase after her. I took my phone, shut the door, and I haven't thought about it until now. Nor did I ever believe she would have the smarts, much less know anyone who would fuck with it."

"The real question is, could she be involved with Lopez?" Channing arched a brow. "And why?"

"Let me contact Mia. I'll also call Bruce, my friend from the DEA." Makenna pulled out her cell and stepped into the hallway.

"See what they have to say, but maybe you and Channing should go have a little chat with her," Talon said.

"Why us?" Marley asked. "You'll get more out of her."

"Stacey hates me." Channing smiled as though he was proud of that fact. "Last time I saw her, she called me a weasel and a snake and reminded me that my girlfriend slept with my brother. Makenna was with me."

"That's a low blow, but that makes Talon the snake." Marley lowered her chin.

"She thought I was Talon," Channing said. "I enjoyed letting her go off on me." He shrugged. "And then I let her have it. That's why I'm a weasel and a snake."

Marley narrowed her eyes. "You purposely misled me."

"To prove I can play Talon as well as he can be me."

"No fighting, children." Talon stood behind her, giving her shoulders a massage. "If Stacey saw us together, she'd certainly have shit to say. But one of us has to stay with our kid."

Marley chewed on that thought for a few minutes.

"Look. I had no idea what Stacey did until this week. Talon and I might not have been on the best of terms. We don't see eye to eye on a lot of things. But we've always had each other's backs. If we need to confront Stacey, this isn't a horrible plan." Channing glanced over his shoulder.

"We've got a problem." Makenna tucked her cell in her back pocket as she stormed into the kitchen. "But before I get into that, this Aegis Network is amazing. In a matter of minutes, we had footage from…" Makenna shook her head. "… doesn't matter. Point is, we have two really big issues we have to address. The first one is Harlon Carter is Stacey's cousin."

"You've got to be kidding me. How did we miss that?" Channing asked.

"Because if it's on her mother's side, which by the last name I suspect it is, Stacey hasn't spoken to anyone from that family since she was a little girl," Talon said. "She never talked about her relatives; honestly, I never asked."

Makenna glanced at her phone. "It's her mother's sister's son, but Mia Sarich has already found intel that shows Stacey with Carter."

"Well, shit," Talon muttered. "This isn't good. What's the second thing we need to be worried about?"

"We have video proof that the girl who was hanging out with Stacey that night she ran into you works for Lopez and was last seen with him in Miami." Makenna pursed her lips.

"Fuck," Marley said under her breath. "Where are they now?"

"As of last night, the Aegis Network lost Lopez

and this Teresa Flicker woman." Channing stared at his brother. "They know we're watching. It's like they are the puppet master and we're dangling from the strings."

"So, they pulled us off our game," Marley said. "It's time we pull them off theirs."

8

"I don't like being sitting ducks like this.
Not when our child is with us." Talon
had been stewing in his own thoughts—marinating
in them—for the last few hours. He'd paced. He'd
read Tallie stories. Watched a show with her and
played war a dozen times. When he wasn't doing
that, Marley was spending time with Tallie and
trying to get a handle on Lopez and Teresa.

"I don't either." Marley handed him a water
bottle, then leaned over and kissed a sleeping Tallie
on the forehead before easing down to the floor. She
leaned into his arm and rested her head on his
shoulder. "I hate admitting this because I trust my
team, but I'd feel a lot better if Channing was
here."

Talon chuckled. "I love that you're using his first name. Does that mean you like him now?"

"I've always liked him." Marley lifted her head. "But I didn't appreciate the dynamic between the two of you or the way he treated you and it got worse after Colombia."

"It wasn't entirely his fault. If I'm being honest with myself, every time he shined, I took that as I'm not as good and I did something to prove it."

"I didn't understand that back then. The way the two of you bounced off each other wasn't healthy. When you added in the situation with Makenna, I resented how hard he was on you," Marley said.

"I deserved it." His heart thumped in the center of his throat. He wasn't used to having support from the people in his life.

"No. You didn't." She palmed his cheek. "It was weird for me to see the three of you being a family, all forgiven. I wanted to hate them for their part in tearing you down and you having to carry the burden for something that was a mistake by two people."

"You're sweet. But that's not what happened." He took her hand and kissed it. "It wasn't easy. Not for any of us," Talon said. "Channing and I have spent a lifetime hurting each other in different ways. But that's over. We've put all that shit behind us."

"I'm glad that you've been able to do that." She smiled. "He and Makenna make a good couple. I shouldn't have been such a bitch to them when I showed up at your parents' house. It wasn't about them as much as it was about me and the fact that I kept Tallie from you."

"It's okay. We all have a lot of history. They sorted out theirs and now it's our turn." He leaned over and pressed his mouth against her warm lips in a slow, tender kiss. He let it linger, tasting and savoring it for as long as he could. This wasn't the time or place for romance. They'd have plenty of time to reconnect as a family when this was all over. "We're going to get through this, and then I'd like to take some time, just the three of us."

"I'd like that," she said. "But I'm really concerned. Lopez knows too much about us. I read and reread that file. The only mole that makes sense would be Carter. He left the DEA two years ago and works for Omega Mission. They take jobs no one else will and many of them are illegal, or they use incredibly unethical methods to get the job done. But the thing that bothers me the most is his connection to Stacey. I didn't see that coming."

"Neither did I. She's always been able to carry a grudge, but this is over the top." Talon sucked in a deep breath, letting it out slowly. "We're both very good at what we do. The best. Anytime I was in the field and knew you would be at the extraction point, I felt a little safer. I believed no matter what, I was getting out alive."

"Are you going to beat us both up for what's happening?"

"No. Just me." It wasn't so much that he planned on kicking himself in the ass. There was no way he could have put all this together because he didn't have all the pieces to the puzzle. Even if he knew about Tallie, he couldn't have known. Lopez was always one step ahead because he had someone feeding him information from the very beginning.

Carter.

"I have a history with Carter and it's not a good one," he admitted.

"Didn't you say that started before the mission nine years ago when we rescued Makenna?" She shifted, sitting cross-legged.

He nodded. "I can understand why Lopez wants to come after me. You. Even Makenna. I don't get Carter. I thought our problems were bullshit testosterone issues. If anyone thought I had control issues, they never worked with Carter."

"I never did an op with him, but I know the problems many have had with him and it all boils down to his inability to follow orders."

Talon tilted his head. "That's kind of been my problem."

"No." She shook her head. "We both struggle with orders that place the mission over people. Anytime we've bent the rules, we've done so only when we've felt not doing it would put our people in danger. Carter has always put mission and heroics first. He cares only about how he's seen and how the outcome will serve him."

"I'm not going to argue any of that." Talon's mind slowly worked at connecting all the dots. There weren't many of them, but now that players and their relationships had begun forming a picture, Talon understood that this entire situation had been nine years in the making. The planning that had to go into it and now the execution put him and everyone else on his side at a huge disadvantage. He and Marley were now playing catch up.

Normally, he could handle that and thrive in the challenge.

He reached behind him and rested his hand on his daughter's ankle. His job now was to keep his family safe. That was his top priority, even if it meant letting others take care of the nitty-gritty.

Marley held his gaze. "We're doing the right thing by drawing Lopez to us."

"I just hope we can get Tallie out before she gets hurt."

"We'll see them coming," Marley said softly. "We have to trust the team we have in place. And we have to rely on each other. She'll be taken to safety and we can take of Lopez, Stacey, and Carter once and for all."

"Marley," Talon whispered. "Wake up. It's time to roll." He reached across the bed and lifted Tallie into his arms. "Hey, sweetie. Time to go for a ride."

Tallie rubbed her eyes as she twisted her little body. "Where are we going, Daddy?"

Marley jumped to her feet without saying a word. She knew the drill. She was a professional. They had made a plan and were as prepared as they could be.

"Charlie is going to take you to see Uncle Channing and Aunt Makenna," Talon said.

"We'll catch up to you in a day or two. Mommy and Daddy have to take care of something first."

"You mean deal with the bad guys." Tallie cupped his face. "I want to stay with you." Her lower lip quivered and her eyes filled with tears.

Broke his damn heart. "I know, baby. I wish you could. But it's too dangerous." Since she knew something was up, he didn't see the point in lying. Not when five feet away, Marley was holstering a weapon to her ankle.

"Promise to be safe and to have Mommy's six?"

"Pinky promise." He held up his hand.

Tallie hooked her pinky with his and tugged.

"Go collect your backpack." He set Tallie on the floor. "And why don't you get the bag of popcorn for the trip."

Tallie brushed her hair from her face and padded from the bedroom to the kitchen.

"Did you get any sleep?" Marley handed him his weapon and his holster.

He strapped it onto his belt. "An hour here and there, but our daughter takes up the entire mattress."

Marley laughed. "I thought it was bad when it was just the two of us, but three was rough."

"What are you talking about? You slept like a baby." He inched closer, taking her by the hips. "Every time I looked over, you were blissfully asleep. That's not like you, or at least the you I remember. You were always a restless sleeper."

"I still am, but a weight was lifted the moment I told you about Tallie and truthfully, even though I know we're not safe, I felt so next to you. The last time I was in that place was when we were together."

"Are you saying what I hope you're saying?"

She dropped her head to his chest and sighed. "I'm scared. I don't want Tallie to be hurt."

He lifted her chin. "I'd be lying if I said this entire thing doesn't freak me right the fuck out. But I've never stopped loving you and from the second I learned about Tallie, I knew I wanted to be a full-time father."

"I still love you too."

Talon's breath got stuck in the center of his chest. He couldn't swallow. He stared into Marley's intense, loving eyes and got lost. Everything that had been upside down in his world, all of a sudden made sense.

"Well, isn't this nice," a male voice with a deep Spanish accent filled the room.

Instinctively, Talon pushed Marley behind his arm.

"Where the fuck is my daughter?" Marley lunged forward, but Talon kept her back.

They needed to keep their cool despite their emotions being at an all-time high.

He tilted his head. He could see a woman who looked vaguely familiar.

Teresa Flicker. Stacey's friend from that night at the bar when he'd lost his cell.

Fuck. She sat there with his daughter at the kitchen counter while Tallie ate a bowl of cereal. Tallie glanced over her shoulder. Her eyes were wide with fear.

Smart girl to know these people were not the good guys.

However, this meant that Charlie had been compromised. Possibly killed. Talon had to think fast so he could get a message to his brother just in case those watching the house hadn't been able to before security had been breached.

"Relax. I'm not a child killer," Lopez said. "I suppose we all have that in common."

"Had I known what kind of man you'd grow

into, maybe I would have made an exception." Talon shouldn't bait someone holding a gun to his head while someone else had a gun only a foot away from his precious baby, but old habits died hard.

Carter strolled into the room.

Talon clenched his fists. His pulse went through the roof. "You're the fucking scum of the earth," he mumbled.

"Did you say something?" Carter smiled, waving a gun in front Marley.

"I think you heard me." Talon's mind kept telling him to shut the fuck up, but his lips wouldn't close.

"Hmmmm." Carter poked him in the center of his chest with the bullet end of his weapon before disarming him and then moving to Marley. It seemed Carter took great joy in patting her down.

Talon gritted his teeth. He was going to make sure Carter paid for that.

"You always rode in on your high horse, believing that you were better than everyone else, but you didn't have the street credentials to back it up." Carter handed the weapons to Lopez, who stepped out of view for a moment.

"His record stands on its own merits. So does

mine. Yours, however, sucks," Marley said, easing from behind Talon. "You were behind Makenna's failed mission. You screwed over her team, my team, and Talon's. You're a traitor and you belong in a military prison. Now, if you will excuse me, I'm going to go make sure my daughter is okay."

"She's fine." Lopez blocked the door. "Teresa's going to take her for a little ride."

"Over my fucking dead body." Talon took a step forward.

Carter raised his weapon. "You're going to die. But do you really want that sweet little girl to witness it?"

Talon's heart dropped to bottom of his stomach.

"You see. I'm not a cold, heartless bastard like you were," Lopez said. "I wouldn't want your little girl to see you, her mother, and the rest of her family perish right in front of her eyes like I had to. I'm not even going to tie you up because I know how traumatizing this all can be for a small child and I want her to be as innocent as possible." Lopez shook his head. "I'm going to make sure she's whisked away to a safe place, and then the two of you and everyone you love will pay for what you did to me." He glanced over his shoulder. "And I'll raise that child right."

"The hell you will." Talon slowed his breath and gripped Marley's hand. They desperately needed to calm their emotions and regroup for the sake of their family. They were getting out of here alive, and so will Tallie, if it was the last thing he ever did.

9

"We can't let her get in that car," Marley whispered.

"I know." Talon stood in the bedroom, facing the window with his hands on his hips.

She peeked out of the room. Tallie sat on the family room floor, hugging her backpack and watching television. She looked utterly terrified with her eyes big, and Marley could tell she wasn't paying any attention to the show. Her gaze kept darting around the room, but to her credit, she didn't budge from her spot while Lopez and his goons sat around the kitchen counter, pointing at a computer screen.

"You're making me crazy just standing there." She inched closer, almost afraid to touch him as she could feel the rage seeping from his skin.

"Sorry, but when Channing and I were kids and I would sneak out, he'd always have my six and we had this signal that it was safe to come in. I'm waiting for that sign."

"What was it?"

"The sound of an owl. I'd hoot three times and pause and then repeat. If it was safe, he'd flicker a light out the window."

"It's broad daylight. We can't do that."

He turned. "But at least I'd know he and the cavalry were here."

"What the hell do you think happened? We had four people outside waiting for them to show up." She inched closer, resting her hands on his biceps. "Everyone in the Aegis Network is as highly trained as you are."

"We have to accept the fact that Lopez and his team have been watching us for a long time. No matter how much we believe we went on the offensive, we're still playing defense." Talon pulled her into his arms and kissed her forehead. "But there is no way they are taking my daughter without having to put a bullet in my body first."

"Mine too." She stiffened.

Hoot. Hoot. Hoot.

Long pause.

Hoot. Hoot. Hoot.

She glanced up. "Did I just hear an owl?"

Talon raised a finger to his lips.

Hoot. Hoot. Hoot.

Long pause.

Hoot. Hoot. Hoot.

"Oh, hell yes." Talon smiled. "We need to be prepared. Now."

"That means we need to go be with our daughter." She arched a brow.

"You go be by her side. Make sure she's away from any windows or doors. Be ready to cover her if you have to, but hopefully, it won't come down to that. Channing is much more cautious in the field than I am, which is good and bad. He'll want every access point covered. He won't come charging in unless that's the only option."

"What are you going to do?" Marley's heart raced. Her blood ran fast and hot. Her number one goal was to ensure her daughter was safe from harm. She knew without a shadow of a doubt that Talon wanted that too. She could see in his eyes how much he'd fallen in love with Tallie and he'd go to the ends of the earth to protect his family.

Marley trusted him with their lives, but sitting on the sidelines wasn't in her nature.

Or taking orders.

"Observe Lopez, Carter, and Teresa. Maybe engage them in conversation. Distract them while we wait for whoever is out there with Channing to make a move or contact us."

"They might find that weird since we've been distant for the last ten minutes."

"They took the phones we had and our weapons." He rubbed his temples. "My only real concern is what they could be communicating to the outside world," Talon said. "We made it clear with my brother what and how'd we'd text, but I still don't trust that Lopez won't manage to get misinformation out there. They might think it stranger that we haven't been trying to talk their ear off."

"All right. But don't piss them off." Marley rose up on tiptoe and kissed his cheek. She took him by the hand and tugged him toward the kitchen.

"Mommy!" Tallie jumped to her feet and raced into Marley's arms. Crocodile tears filled her sweet blue eyes.

"Hey, baby girl. Let's go finish your show." She took Tallie into the family room, which was really an extension of the kitchen, and sat on the floor with her child in her lap. She held her tight. "I love you," she whispered. "Daddy's going to take care of everything." God, she wanted to believe that were true. Deep down, she knew the odds were stacked against them.

Then again, that had been the story of their lives.

Talon had been in worse situations than this, but none of them included someone who had stolen his heart. He had friends who had children and they all told him that kind of love was something so different it couldn't be put into words.

Now he knew exactly what it meant.

"What the hell are we waiting for?" Talon leaned against the counter and stared at Lopez.

"If you must know, we're waiting until we can show you that everyone has been eliminated." Lopez sat on a stool behind a computer. "Your ex-girlfriend, Stacey, hasn't been able to pull off engaging your family, so we're going to have to go a different route."

Talon chuckled. "For starters, I wouldn't call her

an ex and my family hates her, so that's your first mistake."

Lopez narrowed his gaze. "I'm also a bit shocked that your brother is a little more cunning than I expected."

"You should never underestimate a Winston."

Lopez laughed but didn't glance up over his screen or say another word.

Teresa stood at the back door with a weapon on her hip, while Carter kept watch at the front door, his weapon also in a holster. Talon didn't know how many men they had surrounding the small intra-coastal home. It didn't necessarily matter. That was his brother's department today.

Talon glanced at his watch. It had been exactly eleven minutes since he'd heard the owl call.

Lopez kept his gun on the counter, only a fingertip away.

No matter how many times Talon tried to think of a play, he landed on the wrong end of a bullet. He knew he had to be patient.

Not his strong suit.

The cell next to Lopez's computer buzzed. The screen lit up.

"It's your brother," Lopez said, shoving the phone in Talon's direction. "Answer it."

"Why?" Talon narrowed his stare.

"Because I texted him—as you—a while ago and he's finally returning my call."

Let the games begin.

"Keep it on speaker," Lopez said.

"It might help if I knew what you texted." Talon took the cell in his hands.

"You can read it."

Quickly, he pulled up the text string.

Talon: *Call me as soon as you get this. Change in plans.*

Pretty fucking generic. But definitely nothing he would say. Too wordy. Talon would have left it at: *Call me. Plans changed.*

"Hey, bro," Talon said. "Where you at?" Code for: *hurry the fuck up.*

"Just finished getting the family set up in Aunt Betty's rental."

Talon wanted laugh. Aunt Betty didn't have a place she rented out. But at least the family was safe.

Lopez shoved a piece of paper across the table, asking where that was.

"I bet Mom and Dad aren't thrilled about being in that small space with everyone, especially over in Naples. They hate that side of the state."

"I know. But we should be back at the safe house in forty-five," Channing said. "You mentioned a change in plans, but I don't think that's a good idea. Do remember the old owl at the state park?"

"Yeah. I remember." There was no owl. And no park. This all had to do with a signal. And it was up to Talon to understand because his brother couldn't be forty-five minutes away. He had to be close by. He was just buying time.

"Damn thing is still there and driving Aunt Betty batshit. Hoots five times like every fifteen minutes right outside the master bathroom. Swear to God. She wanted Mom and Dad to switch bedrooms."

Talon laughed. His aunt Betty wouldn't give up a master bedroom for anything. Not even a nosy owl. But that wasn't the point. Aunt Betty was code for Tallie.

Once again, Lopez shoved a note under Talon's nose. He rubbed his temple. "Look, bro. Why don't we meet you halfway? I'm getting squirrelly sitting here. I'll text you a location."

"All right. Give me five and then send it."

"Sounds good. See you soon." Talon ended the call, grateful that Marley had heard every word.

"You're not as stupid as I thought you were." Lopez snagged the phone and quickly sent a text.

The one thing Lopez didn't understand about Talon and his twin was they were true to their word whether they were on good terms or not. So, if Channing asked for five minutes, Talon would have waited. He wouldn't have jumped the gun like that. There were a lot of messages sent that had so many meanings, but the most important ones were that Talon and his twin had completely mended their fences once and for all and it felt so good.

Marley checked the time.

Five minutes before something happened. Five minutes before all hell broke loose and either they were saved.

Or they were dead.

But she understood that she needed to get her daughter to the bathroom. That message came out loud and clear.

"Sweetheart, I'm going to need you to do something for me and I'm going to need you to do it now," she whispered in Tallie's ear.

Tallie nodded.

"Ask me to go to the bathroom and once you are in there, I want you to lock the door, lie down in the bathtub, and do not open that door for anyone except me, Daddy, Uncle Channing, or Aunt Makenna. No matter what you hear or how scared you are, don't do it. Do you understand me?"

With a quivering lip, Tallie nodded. "Mommy. I have to go to the bathroom." She sniffled.

"Okay, honey." Marley stood, taking her daughter's hand and walking her to the restroom. "Do you want Mommy to go in with you?"

"No. I'm a big girl." Tallie lifted her chin.

God, Marley hated doing this to her own kid, but she had to remind herself this was for her own protection. Talon was going to need help. Without her, it was three against one on the inside. She checked the time.

Two minutes.

She caught Talon's gaze and held it for a long knowing moment. She chose to stay by the bathroom. She had a clear line of vision to the back door, while Talon had one to the front of the house.

The next couple of minutes were going to be the longest in her life. She'd faced fear more than once. She'd thought she was going to die a few times. But nothing was ever as bad as this.

The bathroom door rattled.

Shit. She shouldn't have asked her child to be that brave. She was only five years old.

Quickly, she turned.

"Mommy. I need help." Tallie opened the door a little.

"Sure." The second she stepped inside, she gasped, staring at Channing.

He pressed his finger to his lips, then handed her two weapons, which she quickly slipped into her jeans, pulling her shirt down to hide them. She knelt down, holding her daughter by the shoulders. "I'm so proud of you," she said softly.

"Makenna is outside the window. Let's get Tallie out of here and take care of this once and for all," Channing whispered.

Marley did her best to keep the tears from rolling down her cheeks. "Be a good girl." She kissed her darling daughter and handed her to Channing who lifted her through the window.

"What happened to Charlie?" Marley asked.

"Wounded badly but not dead," Channing said. "Two others took bullets. One stood down, on my command. I told them unless they saw something, to wait for me. I need you to go back in there and play this out."

Marley nodded and stepped back into the main room.

"Where's your daughter?" Lopez stared.

"She had an accident. I need to get her some fresh clothes. They are in her backpack." Marley squared her shoulders.

"Teresa. Go get the kid her stuff. The rest of us are leaving," Lopez said. "We're going to go meet Channing. Time to bury the bodies."

Marley swallowed. She needed to get to Talon so she could get him the gun that was burning a hole in her back.

"Sure thing, babe." Teresa strolled through the room, running her hand across Lopez's back, kissing him on the cheek as she passed by. "I can't wait for this to be over and we can go back to Colombia. I'm tired of this country."

"You and me both," Lopez said, tapping his fingers against the keyboard. "We'll take the little girl and start our new life."

Marley was surprised by that declaration. Teresa didn't have an accent, but it didn't matter. The tides were about to change. She came up behind Talon, resting her hand on his back. As quickly as she could, she tugged at his slacks, stuffing the weapon in them, adjusting his shirt.

To his credit, he didn't flinch. But he did shift his gaze, tilting his head, as if to ask where that came from, but she could tell he knew his brother was in the house.

Teresa lifted the knapsack off the floor and proceeded to the bathroom where she tapped on the door. "I'm coming in, Tallie."

Marley nodded toward Carter.

Talon blinked once. Meaning he agreed.

Game on.

Teresa tapped on the door.

Marley inched closer to where Carter stood.

Talon reached for the weapon on the counter.

"What the fuck?" Teresa muttered as the bathroom door flew open.

Marley raised her weapon. "Don't move, asshole, or I'll shoot." She kicked the gun from Carter's hand and wrestled him to the floor, taking an elbow to the gut. She could hear struggles in the background; however, she needed to deal with Carter before helping out Talon and Channing.

She groaned, taking a fist to her ribs, but ignored the pain, nailing Carter in the back of the head with the butt of her weapon. He dropped to the floor like a sack of potatoes, out cold. "Piece of shit."

Bang!

"Goddammit. Now that just pisses me off." Talon slammed his free hand on the counter.

"Ticks me off too." Channing came up behind Lopez, jabbing his weapon into his back. "You're going to pay for shooting my twin."

"Talon!" Marley raced to Talon's side as he dropped to his knees, gripping his gut. Blood oozed through his fingers, his face already draining of color.

"I'm fine," he said weakly.

"No. You're not." She took a dish towel and pressed it against his stomach.

Four other men came barreling through the front door, guns drawn. Channing waved them through, barking orders, and they dealt with Lopez, Carter, and Teresa.

"Where's my daughter? Where's Tallie?" Talon managed between a couple of coughs.

Channing knelt next to his twin. "She's a few blocks away with Makenna. She's safe." Channing tapped his ear. "I need an ambulance, now."

"Lie down." Marley sucked in a deep breath and allowed all her military training to take over. She ripped at Talon's shirt and assessed the wound.

The blood came fast and it was warm, as if it was coming straight from the heart.

"It's not that bad." Talon palmed her cheek. "I've been injured worse. Shot more times. This is nothing."

"It better be nothing because we have a future to discuss and our daughter needs her father." She leaned over and kissed his forehead. "I need you too." But she knew his wound wasn't nothing and the love of her life was in real trouble.

10

*T*alon leaned against the front porch railing of Marley's house in Orlando with his hand over his wound. It had been two weeks since he'd been shot, and his stomach still ached. It took a five-hour surgery to remove the bullet from his gut. He'd been damn fucking lucky it missed all his important organs. He'd lost a lot of blood, but Channing was there and didn't hesitate to donate whatever was necessary.

Talon spent another three days in the hospital to recover. Tallie and Marley didn't leave his side until he was discharged. Then he spent a week at home with his parents. His aunt Betty waited on him like he was a prince.

That was new and oddly strange, but he enjoyed

her company. She told him stories of his childhood and kept him from going crazy. She was also the one who fed him the news that Stacey had been arrested.

He wasn't sure how he felt about that one. She'd been used. Lopez played on her emotions, but her sentence would be light and hopefully she learned her lesson.

During his stay at his parents, he spoke to his daughter and Marley every day and FaceTimed with them as much as possible. He wished they could be with him, but Tallie had missed so much school and Marley did have a job.

He also wasn't ready to introduce them to his family. He needed time to heal and they needed to bond as a family.

He'd arrived in Orlando early this morning so he could spend the rest of his medical leave with his daughter.

And reconnect with Marley.

"Are you okay?" Marley stepped outside and handed him a beer. "You've been really quiet ever since you got here, but especially since Tallie went to bed."

He sat down on the top step and sipped. He

needed to pick his words carefully. He didn't want to scare her away. They had danced around so many topics since he'd been shot. The only thing they had come to terms with was that Tallie needed them both. Marley planned to move to Jacksonville to work there at the Aegis Network office in six weeks.

His contract with the Army ended in five months and he hadn't signed the re-enlistment contract. If things went as planned today, he had no intention of putting his John Hancock on that piece of paper.

"Talon, I hate it when you're this contemplative. It makes me crazy because I can't tell what you're thinking." She sat down next to him and leaned against his shoulder.

He chuckled.

"It's not funny. You only get quiet when there's bad news. You're always so quick to react, so this shit scares the crap out of me."

"I'm sorry. I don't mean to laugh." He squeezed her knee. "I love you and Tallie and I want us to be a family."

"We are one."

He shook his head. "I want Tallie to have my last name."

"I know she'd love that and I'm certainly good with it. We can make that happen."

"Not just on paper." He stretched out his legs. This wasn't going quite as planned. No one could ever call him Mr. Romance. They hadn't dated in years. They got tossed into a crazy situation, but it was as if they'd never stopped being together.

"I'm not sure I follow."

"I want you to have my last name."

"Excuse me?" She jerked her head back. "What are you saying?"

His fingers—no, his entire hand—shook with a combination of fear and excitement as he pulled out a small emerald ring. It wasn't the traditional engagement ring, but there was nothing traditional about Marley. Besides, she loved emeralds. It had always been her favorite stone. She didn't wear jewelry often, but when she did, she loved it more if it had an emerald in it.

"I want us to get married and work together at the Aegis Network."

Her eyes grew wide and her lips parted. She stared at the ring. "Holy shit, that's a lot to process." Tentatively, she took the ring in her fingers. "You're not re-enlisting?"

"I want to be a full-time father. I don't want to

miss another minute. My job as a ranger would take me away too much from Tallie and from you. I love you both so much that even these last few days of being apart hurt my heart."

Marley held the ring up in the moonlight before placing it on her finger. "It hurt me too." She palmed his cheek. "I love you with all my soul. I'm sorry I took so much away—"

"Shhh… that's all in the past." He kissed her sweet lips. "We have the chance at a fresh start. I want to take it and run with it."

"So do I."

"Is that a yes?"

"Oh, hell yes," Marley said with a big smile. "On one condition."

"What's that?"

"We have another child sometime in the near future."

He set his beer on the step, jumped to his feet, and lifted her in his arms. He swallowed his groan and ignored the pain from his wound.

"What the hell are you doing?"

"No time like the present to start working on that project."

EPILOGUE

TWO WEEKS LATER...

Talon lifted a shaky finger and let it hover over his parents' home doorbell. He glanced down at his daughter, who held her mother's hand, looking up at him with a big smile and excited eyes. "Remember what Mommy and Daddy said."

"I won't say word." Tallie raised her fingers to her mouth and ran them across her lips as if to zip them shut.

Talon let out a long breath. He still couldn't bring himself to ring the bell.

"I'm the one who should be afraid. Not you," Marley whispered. "I know what Makenna went through after your uncle Henry's funeral. Your aunt

Betty can be brutal. I'm sure she's going to have a few words for me."

"She's going to forgive you in five seconds because of Tallie. She'll be thrilled that we wanted to get married. She will wring my neck for eloping. My mother will too. They never thought that I would ever settle down or have a family. I was always such a disappointment to them. While part of them will be happy, I can already see and hear the judgment."

"Stop. You've always believed you live in Channing's shadow, but some of that is on you. Tallie and I need you to go into this with your head held high. Your family is going to be fine with this."

Talon pressed the button. He sucked in a deep breath and held it, counting backward from ten.

The door swung open. His father stood in the center of the door with the damn fucking scowl he always sported. The man was never happy. He was impossible to please. Even perfect Channing struggled for approval from their father. They both knew he loved them, but Rupert could be a tough read.

"Hey, Dad. You remember Marley."

"Hi, Rupert," Marley said. "It's good to see you again."

"We're happy you're here." His dad nodded.

"My son tells me that the two of you are back together as a couple."

"Yes, sir. We are," Marley said.

"That's good. I'm glad Talon has someone like you in his life. If anyone can keep him in line, it's you." His father's eyes went right to Tallie. He bent down. "You must be my granddaughter, Tallie."

Tallie nodded like a bobblehead. "I am." She smiled, holding out her hand. "It's nice to meet you."

"How about we hug." His father opened his arms, pulling Tallie in for a big squeeze. He lifted her feet right off the front porch. "Why don't we go into the family room? Do you like the game concentration?"

"It's one of my favorites," Tallie said.

His father laughed. "Your dad and uncle Channing could play that all day long when they were your age." He lifted her up and carried her inside. "We're going to have a lot of fun getting to know each other."

"What should I call you?" Tallie asked.

"Grandpa works, if that's okay."

"I like that." Tallie cupped his cheeks and gave him a kiss. "Grandpa."

He tossed his head back and laughed. And smiled. He actually looked happy.

"Who is that man, and what did he do with my dad?" Talon glanced at Marley.

"See. It's all going to be fine."

Talon sighed. "They don't know we're married yet. That we took away their right to see us tie the knot."

"Well, well, well," Aunt Betty's voice landed on his ears like scalding water. "Get in here and let's have a chat."

Shit. "Hello, Aunt Betty," he said. "This is Marley."

"I remember." Aunt Betty looked her up and down. "I should hate you and tell you to get your scrawny ass out of this house, but you bring a precious child, so I'm going to forgive you for your past transgressions. But don't you dare upset this family again." She waggled her finger. "You better not break my Talon's heart."

Talon laughed. He couldn't help it. In all his life, no one had ever been worried about his feelings that way. It had always been the other way around. It was kind of nice for a change. "You don't have to worry about that, Aunt Betty." Behind his back, he fiddled with his wedding ring. "Is everyone else here?"

"Where is that grandbaby of mine?" His mom came running into the family room, wiping her hands on her apron. "I can't believe I had to wait this long to meet her."

"Hello, Mother." Talon smiled. He tugged his mom in for a hug and a kiss. "I didn't mean to keep her from you, but we needed some alone time together."

His mom palmed his cheek before turning to Marley. "I was mad at you." She took Marley by the hands. "But I want to start fresh."

"That means a lot to me." Marley smiled. "I'm sorry for what I did."

"Hush. It's in the past. In this family, we move forward."

In a matter of seconds, the room filled with Channing, Makenna, and his sister Charlette and her family. Charlette had two kids, one of which was a little girl about the same age as Tallie and they hit it off splendidly. Talon's heart was filled with the kind of love and appreciation he'd been looking for his entire life.

Ironically, he'd always had it; he simply hadn't embraced it.

He sat on the sofa, sipping bourbon and watching his daughter play with her cousins. Marley snuggled next to him with a glass of wine. So far, no one had noticed their matching rings, but it had only been an hour. However, if he didn't tell them, he risked Tallie spilling the beans, and then he'd be toast. He cleared his throat. "Can I have everyone's attention, please?"

The room quickly silenced, and all eyes were on him, including the children.

His heart lurched to his throat. His pulse soared. His family might have accepted his daughter. And Marley. That was the easy part. But marriage? Without them being a part of it? That was a different story.

"Marley and I have an announcement." He took her hand and squeezed. "We got married last week."

"Yeah. We saw the rings," his father said with a wave of his hand as if it were old news. "We all were wondering when you would finally get the nerve to tell us."

"Aunt Betty has been putting together a guest list for the last forty minutes for a belated reception party." His mother sat on the floor with Edwin, Charlette's youngest child in her lap, playing patty-cake. Tears welled in her eyes. "We're all so happy for you. We can see how much your soul has settled and what the two of you mean to each other."

"I can't believe he got married before me. Had a kid before me. You stole my thunder, bro," Channing said. "Now I'm one step behind you."

"It's about time Talon got the spotlight and not because he screwed up," Aunt Betty said with a wicked grin. She winked. "Perhaps the tide's are changing."

"Never." Channing downed his drink. "Not on my watch. Hoot. Hoot."

Talon burst out laughing. He wrapped his arm around his wife.

Wife.

His life had taken a huge turn and he couldn't wait to see what was around the corner.

Thank you so much for taking the time to read TALON'S HONOR. Please feel free to leave an honest review.

Don't forget to check out Kendal Talbot's book, **DELTA MISSION.**

If you'd like to know more about the AEGIS

NETWORK, please visit my website: https://jentalty.com/the-aegis-network/

Sign up for my Newsletter (https://dl.bookfunnel.com/82gm8b9k4y) where I often give away free books before publication.

Join my private Facebook group (https://www.facebook.com/groups/191706547909047/) where I post exclusive excerpts and discuss all things murder and love!

ABOUT THE AUTHOR

Jen Talty is the *USA Today* Bestselling Author of Contemporary Romance, Romantic Suspense, and Paranormal Romance. In the fall of 2020, her short story was selected and featured in a 1001 Dark Nights Anthology.

Regardless of the genre, her goal is to take you on a ride that will leave you floating under the sun with warmth in your heart. She writes stories about broken heroes and heroines who aren't necessarily looking for romance, but in the end, they find the kind of love books are written about :).

She first started writing while carting her kids to one hockey rink after the other, averaging 170 games per year between 3 kids in 2 countries and 5 states. Her first book, IN TWO WEEKS was originally published in 2007. In 2010 she helped form a publishing company (Cool Gus Publishing) with *NY*

Times Bestselling Author Bob Mayer where she ran the technical side of the business through 2016.

Jen is currently enjoying the next phase of her life…the empty nester! She and her husband reside in Jupiter, Florida.

Grab a glass of vino, kick back, relax, and let the romance roll in…

Sign up for my Newsletter (https://dl.bookfunnel.com/ 82gm8b9k4y) where I often give away free books before publication.

Join my private Facebook group (https://www.facebook. com/groups/191706547909047/) where I post exclusive excerpts and discuss all things murder and love!

Never miss a new release. Follow me on Amazon:amazon.com/author/jentalty

And on Bookbub: bookbub.com/authors/jen-talty

ALSO BY JEN TALTY

Brand new series: SAFE HARBOR!

Mine To Keep

Mine To Save

Mine To Protect

Mine to Hold

Mine to Love

Check out LOVE IN THE ADIRONDACKS!

Shattered Dreams

An Inconvenient Flame

The Wedding Driver

Clear Blue Sky

Blue Moon

Before the Storm

NY STATE TROOPER SERIES (also set in the Adirondacks!)

In Two Weeks

Dark Water

Deadly Secrets

Murder in Paradise Bay

To Protect His own

Deadly Seduction

When A Stranger Calls

His Deadly Past

The Corkscrew Killer

First Responders: A spin-off from the NY State Troopers series

Playing With Fire

Private Conversation

The Right Groom

After The Fire

Caught In The Flames

Chasing The Fire

Legacy Series

Dark Legacy

Legacy of Lies

Secret Legacy

Emerald City

It's all in the Whiskey

Johnnie Walker

Georgia Moon

Jack Daniels

Jim Beam

Whiskey Sour

Whiskey Cobbler

Whiskey Smash

Irish Whiskey

The Monroes

Color Me Yours

Color Me Smart

Color Me Free

Color Me Lucky

Color Me Ice

Color Me Home

Search and Rescue

Protecting Ainsley

Protecting Clover

Protecting Olympia

THE AEGIS NETWORK

The Sarich Brother

The Lighthouse

Her Last Hope

The Last Flight

The Return Home

The Matriarch

Aegis Network: Jacksonville Division

A SEAL's Honor

Aegis Network Short Stories

Max & Milian

A Christmas Miracle

Spinning Wheels

Holiday's Vacation

Special Forces Operation Alpha

Burning Desire

Burning Kiss

Burning Skies

Burning Lies

Burning Heart

Burning Bed

Remember Me Always

The Brotherhood Protectors

Out of the Wild

Rough Justice

Rough Around The Edges

Rough Ride

Rough Edge

Rough Beauty

The Brotherhood Protectors

The Saving Series

Saving Love

Saving Magnolia

Saving Leather

Hot Hunks

Cove's Blind Date Blows Up

My Everyday Hero – Ledger

Tempting Tavor

Malachi's Mystic Assignment

Needing Neor

www.ingramcontent.com/pod-product-compliance
Lightning Source LLC
Chambersburg PA
CBHW011519100726
47899CB00010BD/3439